Death at Hilliard High

A Susan Lombardi Mystery

Carole B. Shmurak

★SterlingHouse Publisher, Inc.   Pittsburgh, PA

Death at Hilliard High

PEMBERTON

ISBN-10: 1-56315-454-4
ISBN-13: 978-1-56-315454-6
Trade Paperback
© Copyright 2009 Carole B. Shmurak
All Rights Reserved
Library of Congress #2009922487

Requests for information should be addressed to:
SterlingHouse Publisher, Inc.
3468 Babcock Boulevard
Pittsburgh, PA 15237
info@sterlinghousepublisher.com
www.sterlinghousepublisher.com

Pemberton Mysteries
is an imprint of SterlingHouse Publisher, Inc.

Cover Design: Brandon M. Bittner
Interior Design: Kathleen M. Gall

Printed in U.S.A.

NOTE TO THE READER

There is no town of Hilliard in the state of Connecticut, nor is there a Hilliard High School. The faculty and students described herein are products of my imagination. Metropolitan University and Wintonbury Academy for Girls are also fictitious, as are the towns of Albion and Wintonbury. Nonetheless, some of the incidents described are based on events that happened in Connecticut and Staten Island, New York.

ACKNOWLEDGMENTS

First and foremost, I would like to thank the members of my writing group (Amanda Niedbala, Tom Ratliff, Steve Shmurak, Steve Thomson and Heidi Ulrich) for all of their suggestions and support. I am especially indebted to Amanda for allowing me to spend a day as her shadow. Thanks to Neil Bernstein for technical information, to Phyllis Katz and Jacqueline Baker for advice, and to Johnathan Henninger and Kris Archambault for the use of their names. A big thank you to Chris Demorro for his help with the car club and to Karen Riem for being my eBay guru. My sincere appreciation also goes to Arthur Sher, M.D., for the tale he told at our high school reunion and to Susannah Shmurak for her insights into *Puddn'head Wilson*. And as always, my eternal gratitude to my husband, Steve Shmurak, for his unswerving support and sense of humor.

CAST OF CHARACTERS

AT METROPOLITAN UNIVERSITY:

Susan Lombardi: professor of education, former teacher at Wintonbury Academy for Girls (WAG)

Nanette Lehman: chair of the department of education

AT HILLIARD HIGH SCHOOL:

Shauna Thompson: English teacher, graduate of WAG and Yale University

Amelia Rafferty, Leonard Loops: members of the English department

Jonah Gordon, Georgia Macandrew, Marianna Landino, Brett Altman: members of the history department

Silas Warner: school custodian

Gabe Naughton, Hayden Norris, Alyssa Loeb, Megan Hollister: seniors

Zach Reiner, Kathryn Brooks, Travis Melton, Jenna Lewis, Dave Ryan, Brittany Caruso, Jeff Levine: juniors

ALSO IN THE TOWN OF HILLIARD:

Louise Loops: Leo's wife

Kris Archambault: police officer

Officer Murphy, Officer Foster: other members of the Hilliard Police Department

Mrs. Truesdale: Hilliard Historical Society volunteer, guide at the Winthrop House

Henry McQuillan: clerk in the Records Office at Town Hall

ELSEWHERE:

Michael Buckler: Susan's husband

Elaine Dodgson: teacher of drama at WAG and Susan's best friend

Jon Henninger: author and Elaine's current lover

CHAPTER ONE

It all started with a phone call, a simple, innocent phone call. But I should have learned by then that when my friend Elaine Dodgson called, nothing was ever simple. And seldom innocent.

"Susan, I need a small favor," she began in her cheerful, melodious voice — a voice that had won her several major roles in off-Broadway shows two decades ago.

"Sure," I replied with more certainty than I felt. I stared out of my office window, thinking of some of the favors Elaine had asked for in the past. Helping her return a book she'd stolen from her former headmistress and hiring a private detective to tail her current boyfriend were the ones that came to mind.

"Do you remember Shauna Thompson?"

I remembered her immediately. Shauna had been a student of Elaine's at Wintonbury Academy for Girls, one of the few African-American girls at the school. Six feet tall with blazing eyes and an infectious grin, Shauna was a formidable presence even as a sixteen year old.

"Of course," I said. "She was one of your best drama students."

"And she helped you catch a murderer," Elaine reminded me.

I didn't need the reminder. "What's Shauna doing now?" I asked. "Is she in college?"

"Just graduated from Yale," Elaine replied. "And teaching English at Hilliard High School."

"Yale and Hilliard. That's a pretty impressive résumé."

"Well, you may remember that's she's quite an impressive young woman. But she's run into some problems at Hilliard and I thought you might be able to help her."

"Problems?" I repeated. "Problems with her teaching?"

"Not exactly...."

"But what sort of problems then? And why do you think I might help her?"

"I think it would be best if Shauna explained it to you herself. Will you be home tonight? And can she give you a call?"

"Sure," I said, my curiosity now roused. "I'd love to hear from her."

"You're fabulous. Thanks, Susan. See you next Tuesday!"

I hung up the phone and looked at my watch. It was nearing the end of my office hours, and no students were waiting for me in the hallway. After shuffling some papers around on my desk for a few more minutes, I locked my office, said goodbye to Marie, the education department secretary, and hurried to my car through the chilly September rain.

* * * * *

"Swash, I'm home!" I called as I came in the door.

There was no answer. I wondered if he were asleep in front of the TV set — a highly unusual occurrence at this time of day — and tiptoed into the family room to see. No Swash. A spicy aroma was wafting through the kitchen so I knew he had to be somewhere nearby. I hurried downstairs to our shared study. No Swash there either, though the pile of papers strewn all over the floor indicated recent occupancy.

You have to know Swash to understand how unusual it was not to find him at home. About twenty years ago, he had inherited a fortune from his maiden aunt and started investing it. Soon after, he was able to quit his job entirely. He took up gourmet cooking and reading books about finance, and over the years, Swash left the house less and less often. With the growth of the Internet, he discovered that he could even order groceries online — including the specialty foods he was so particular about — and have them delivered. Aside from the occasional restaurant meal or big screen movie, Swash had no reason or desire to go very far.

"Aha!" I said to myself. "Maybe he's out back picking tomatoes." Usually Swash left that job to me, but he might have needed them for tonight's dinner and couldn't wait for my return home.

I hurried to the garden, but no Swash. With rain dripping onto my hair and trickling down my cheeks, I felt pretty forlorn. *Well, as long as I'm already drenched I might as well do something useful,* I thought. Pulling a couple of Brandywines off the nearest plant, I started to go back inside. Then I heard a noise that seemed to come from the garage.

"Swash!" I called.

"Out here," came the reply.

"There you are," I began, and gasped. "What's *that?*"

"Ah, the prodigal wife returns!" he said. "A somewhat bedraggled prodigal wife, I see. I hope you're in the mood for tandoori chicken tonight."

"Swash, what is that?" I repeated.

"That, m'dear, is a 1957 Chevy Bel Air. Isn't she a beauty?"

CHAPTER TWO

"Well, she — it — certainly is shiny," I said, still in a state of shock. I ran my hand lightly over the powder-blue body. "And all that chrome...."

"Yup," Swash said with a grin. "Biggest grille they ever put on a Chevy."

"Where did you get it?" I asked, hoping perhaps he had only borrowed it from someone.

"Online of course. Collectorcarsonline-dot-com, to be specific."

"But Swash, what will you do with it?"

"Well, I'll admire it a lot. Keep it clean and polished. Maybe I'll drive it around the block now and then."

"But why?"

"Because I wanted one." The grin widened. "And we can afford it. Now are you ready for some tandoori chicken?"

"When am I not ready for tandoori chicken?" I replied as Swash closed up the garage and we headed back inside the house.

I probably should explain a few more things about

Swash. First of all, his name: his doting parents, Adele and Stuart Buckler, had originally named him Michael. Swash was the ironic name that his college buddies had bestowed on him during freshman year in college. Swash and I have been together a long, long time, and we have a daughter, Joanne, who finished college herself not long ago and is currently making her way in the competitive world of investment banking. Buying this car was totally out of character for him, and I wondered if it was the sign of a delayed midlife crisis of some sort.

Savoring the last mouthful of basmati rice, I raised the topic of the car once more. We'd already thoroughly discussed my day and Elaine's requested favor.

"Why a Chevy Bel Air?" I asked. "Why 1957?"

"I don't know exactly. This is what cars looked like when I was little. I just always wanted one."

"They do make little model cars that you could buy, you know," I said. "You could have bought one of those online, put it on your desk, and admired it whenever you wanted to."

"That's not the same," he replied. "Besides I am going to drive it eventually."

"But where will you keep your Honda?" Swash had a little Civic, about ten years old, that he used for his infrequent forays out of the house.

"Oh, I parked that behind the garage. It won't be an eyesore, don't worry."

I was about to reply when the phone in the kitchen

rang. As we always did around supper hour, we let the answering machine take the call.

"Dr. Lombardi?" said the caller. "This is Shauna Thompson. Remember me?"

Remember her? I could practically see her and her Cheshire cat grin in front of me.

"Ms. Dodgson said I could call you...."

After an approving nod from Swash, I picked up the handset. "Hi Shauna," I said. "I was expecting your call a bit later, but this is fine. What's up?"

"Oh, I'm glad you're there. I hate playing phone tag."

"Me too. So you're at Hilliard High, I hear. Is there some problem?"

"Not a problem exactly. My classes are going fine. I'm teaching English, by the way, and I hope to help with the drama productions later in the year."

"Sounds great, Shauna. So, the not-exactly-a-problem is...."

"Yeah, I was getting to that. It's just that there are some strange things going on — strange and disturbing — and I don't really have anyone to talk to about it."

"Well, I'm glad to help, but what would you like me to do?"

"You're an educational consultant, right? You visit schools all the time. So if I told my department chair that I knew you and wanted to have you visit, it wouldn't seem too weird?"

"I guess not," I said.

"I just need another pair of eyes and ears for a day or so — someone to tell me if this is what happens to all first-year teachers and I'm just being paranoid, or if something's really not right...."

Everything I knew about Shauna told me that it took more than a little student misbehavior to upset her. I agreed to spend the day with Shauna at Hilliard High School the following Thursday, the day of the week that I reserved for research and consulting. Surely this visit would qualify as one of those.

CHAPTER THREE

*Our mission is to educate students
for active membership in a complex world.
We teach them to use their minds well
so they may become informed and honest
participants in their community
and in a democratic society.*

— from the Mission Statement of
Hilliard High School, Hilliard, Connecticut

The town of Hilliard, once a sleepy little farming village, boasted more new million-dollar homes than any of the other upscale suburbs of Hartford. Its high school was always at the top of the state rankings, and, in a state where a school district's standardized test scores translated into real estate values, the citizens of Hilliard meant to keep it that way.

I'd been to Hilliard High once or twice over the

past eight years when I'd visited student teachers working there, but now, as I turned my car into its parking lot, I took a fresh look. The old wing of the school, a prime example of schoolhouse gothic with its pointed arches and soaring spires, had been built, according to its cornerstone, in 1920. The new wing, a low-slung structure of glass and brick, was clearly a product of the last baby boomlet. No attempt had been made by the architect to blend the two discordant elements. Maybe, I thought, it was a reflection of how the Hilliard old-timers felt about the upwardly mobile newcomers who had surged into their valley town in the last decade.

I parked my little Toyota in the visitors' lot and immediately wished I'd taken it to the carwash over the weekend. On one side of it, a Mercedes and a BMW gleamed in the sunlight. On the other, three gigantic SUVs glistened — visiting parent volunteers, I assumed.

I followed signs to the main office and was greeted there by a smiling secretary.

"Oh, Ms. Thompson is expecting you," she said when I introduced myself. "Just sign the visitors' book and you can go right to her classroom. It's room 208, just up that stairway and make a right. You'll see it. First period's almost over, so wait till the bell rings before you go in."

I did as I was told, and I soon found myself outside room 208. Peering through the closed glass door, I saw Shauna in front of her class. She was a tall woman with broad shoulders, and she moved with grace as she paced back and forth, gesturing as she spoke to her class. The bell rang, and a large group of fashionably dressed and carefully coiffed adolescents burst from the room. I waited for the last straggler to amble out into the hall and then entered the classroom.

"Dr. Lombardi! Hey, thanks for coming. Those were my freshmen who just left. My juniors will be here in a minute or two." She gave me a warm smile. "I really like my juniors — you'll see how smart they are."

"Good to see you, Shauna," I replied, shaking her proffered hand. "Before they get here, tell me: is there anything special you want me to focus on?"

"Not really. I want your unbiased eye. Just sit back here and see if you spot anything strange, okay? After this class, I've got a free period and I'll explain more then."

Students started to trickle in, and I settled into the chair in the back of the room that Shauna had indicated. I watched carefully as the students entered: boys in loose-fitting T-shirts, khakis and expensive running shoes, girls in brightly colored T-shirts and jeans, with long straight hair falling to their shoulders and flip-flops on their feet. All of them were slim and smiling, with perfect complexions. A few still had braces on their teeth.

Shauna introduced me to the class and started quickly by distributing photocopies of a poem. The students, obviously well-trained even this early in the year, got into groups to discuss the poem and answer the questions that Shauna had written on the whiteboard. The room was soon filled with adolescent chatter and giggling. I wandered around, listening in on their conversations. Accustomed to visitors, the students acknowledged my presence with smiles or nods but went on with their assigned task.

"It's about death," one of the girls said. "Poems are always about death." She had dark brown hair that she kept pushing out of her eyes.

"No, I don't think so," responded another, a petite girl with white-blonde hair and dark blue eyes fringed with white lashes.

Across the room, I saw one dark-haired boy get so excited about what he was saying that he jumped out of his chair.

"That's gross!" exclaimed one of the girls in his group.

Shauna hurried over to them and asked a few questions. The boy sat down again, and the conversation continued more calmly than before.

She approached a group of four boys. I noticed that one of the boys, small for his age and wearing a Red Sox baseball cap, was looking around, uninvolved, and playing with his pen.

"What's your evidence for that?" she asked, pointing at something one of the boys had written in his notebook. Her question caught the attention of the distracted boy and he drew closer to the others in the group. After a few moments, she moved on.

"Okay, guys," Shauna said about twenty minutes later. "You have just a few more minutes. Put a star next to the three best things you have to say about the poem."

The rest of the class was spent with students explaining their ideas and Shauna jotting them on the board. There was some agreement between groups and a lot of lively discussion of their different interpretations. When class was over, the students gathered up their books and zoomed out the door.

"So what did you think?" asked Shauna.

"Good group," I said. "You handle them like a pro."

"Thanks," she said, looking pleased. "Now walk around the room and see if you notice anything strange."

"Strange?" I repeated.

"Just look."

I strolled around the room, gazing at movie posters and portraits of women writers. I scanned the computers at the side of the room and the bookshelves in the back.

"Oh, that's funny," I said. "All the books on your shelves are upside down."

"Look again," she suggested.

I looked. "Hmmm. There *are* a few right side up. Toni Morrison, Alice Walker, Richard Wright, James Baldwin...."

"Do you think someone is trying to tell me something?" she asked.

CHAPTER FOUR

"So all the white writers' books are upside down and only the black writers...."

"Some kind of racist message, you think?" she asked with a crooked smile. I couldn't tell if she was upset and covering it up well or actually somewhat amused.

"Well, it's certainly *about* race," I replied. "Does that make it racist?"

"Yeah, I think so. I think they're trying to tell me that I only know how to teach about black authors. Or maybe that I *should* only teach about black authors — I don't know. Do you think I should tell someone about it? The principal maybe?"

"What's he like?"

"Nice guy. Kind of ineffectual though, according to faculty room gossip."

I thought about it for a few moments. "What about your department chair?"

Shauna shrugged. "That's Amelia Rafferty. I don't know if I should talk to her. She's smart and I think she's a good teacher, but I'm not sure she likes me."

"Well, she helped hire you, right?"

"Yeah, but maybe they just needed a person of color in the school, and I was it."

"How long ago did this happen?" I asked. "And has there been anything else?"

"Well, this happened a few days ago, the day before I called you. Before that, there was a caricature of me drawn on the whiteboard, but I couldn't tell if it was supposed to be insulting or complimentary, so I just erased it."

"Shauna, I think you should show this to your chair, and see what she thinks. And take a photo or two of the shelves as they are now. But I wouldn't make an issue of it with the principal at this point. It's probably just a stupid adolescent prank."

"I hope so," she said. "I guess it's someone's idea of testing the new teacher, huh?" She smiled uncertainly. "I need a cup of coffee. Let's go to the faculty lounge."

Shauna led me down a flight of stairs and into the faculty hideaway. It was a well-lit room, furnished with comfortable old sofas and tall potted plants, as well as several formica-topped tables and mismatched chairs. Two coffeepots and three microwave ovens sat on a long counter alongside a basket of blueberry muffins. At one of the tables, four young faculty members sat, sipping coffee and chatting.

"Hey, Shauna," said one of the men, looking up at us.

"Hi Jonah," she replied. "Dr. Lombardi, this is…."

"Jonah," I said. "Jonah Gordon?" I recognized the intelligent face of one of my former students.

"Hey, Dr. Lombardi. I wondered if you'd remember me."

"Sure, I do. American history?"

"I'm impressed," he said. "What do you have? Two hundred students every year?"

"Yes," I said, "but they don't all write their lesson plans in iambic pentameter."

"It's good to be remembered for the right things," he acknowledged, his dark eyes smiling. "Meet my partners in crime in the history department. This is Georgia, Marianna, and Brett."

"I'm happy to meet you all," I said. "Wow, you're a young department. All new hires?"

"No," said the woman he'd introduced as Georgia. "We've all been here a couple of years." She was a curly-haired redhead who looked young enough to be a teenager herself. Only her long skirt and high-heeled boots distinguished her from the more casually dressed Hilliard students.

"And we do have a few old-timers in the department," added Brett, a darkly handsome man with the build of a football player. "Shauna's the only new kid on the block."

"Yeah, only the English position made the budget this year," Marianna said. "You two want to sit down?"

She indicated the vacant chairs at the table with a wave of her hand — a hand decorated with a huge diamond ring, I noticed.

I looked at Shauna.

"No," she said. "I think I'll give Dr. Lombardi a tour of the school. We'll just get some coffee and head out. But I'll see you all at lunch."

Shauna took down two ceramic mugs from a shelf and handed me one. We filled them with strong-smelling coffee and decided to split a blueberry muffin. Newly fortified, we waved goodbye to the history four-some.

"This way's the cafeteria," said Shauna, indicating a long hallway. "The kids go there during their free periods."

"Study hall in the caf?" I asked.

"Well, the ninth graders have study hall. The others can go there and then sign out to the library or a teacher. Some of them seem to find a way to roam around, some even manage to get out of the building. It's kind of loose."

"So it wouldn't be hard for one of them to get into your room and rearrange the shelves?" I asked.

"I lock the room when I leave," she replied. "But I might forget once in a while."

As we were passing the cafeteria with its familiar noises and smells, a tall, stoop-shouldered man came out of a stairwell.

"Morning, Leo," Shauna said.

He nodded at her. "Good morning, Ms. Thompson." He walked past us and into the cafeteria.

"He's in my department," explained Shauna. "Leo Loops. He's a Hilliard High legend — been here forever."

"Loops?"

"Yeah, the kids all call him 'Loopy.' Not to his face, of course."

"Kind of shabby for Hilliard High, isn't he?"

"Ah, but it's genteel shabbiness," she said. "According to Amelia, the Loopses are an old Hilliard family — they practically founded the town. And Leo went to Princeton. He came back after college, married his high school sweetheart, got a job teaching English here and never left."

We'd arrived at a set of glass doors at the end of the hallway, where the old and new parts of the building met.

"What's beyond those doors?" I asked.

"Principal's office," replied Shauna. "College advisors and counselors' offices. The whole first floor of the old wing is the administrators' domain."

"And the other floors?"

"Classrooms — mostly foreign languages and art and music. Science and math are in the new wing, and English and history too. My room is actually at the corner where the old and new wings meet."

"Is it? I lose all sense of direction when I'm inside a building. And where does that stairway go?" I asked, pointing at a dingy door with a barely readable sign saying 'Stairs' on it.

"Some kind of basement, I guess. I've never been there, to tell the truth. The new wing doesn't have a basement at all."

"Should we go find out what's down there?" I suggested.

Shauna pushed the door open. "Strange that it's not locked," she said. "I guess someone forgot." She stuck her head through the opening and flicked a light switch. "Yuck, it smells kind of damp. And it's not very well-lit."

"If this were a horror movie, the audience would be yelling at us not to go down there," I said.

"Well, maybe we should listen to the audience," she replied.

"Oh, let's just have a peek. You've got some time till your next class, right?"

"Yeah, I suppose it wouldn't hurt…."

We tip-toed cautiously down the stairs.

"Looks like old furniture storage," Shauna said, peering around. "Just a bunch of old desks and chairs."

"Yes," I agreed. "Nothing very interesting, huh?"

"If you were hoping for some dead bodies, I guess you're disappointed."

We returned to the first floor. Shauna did some

photocopying in a small room that held only a copy machine and two desks. Then we strolled through the rest of the new wing, past groups of students retrieving books from lockers and hastily copying each other's homework.

"It's about time for me to get back to my classroom," Shauna said.

"Okay. Time for your seniors now? Chaucer, is it?"

"Yeah, another of those dead white guys," she said. "But I kind of like him. And my Middle English rocks."

CHAPTER FIVE

*We expect each student to become
a skilled thinker who can use a variety of
strategies to create knowledge from information
and acquire understanding
from experience.*

— from the Mission Statement of
Hilliard High School

When we arrived back at Shauna's classroom, there was an envelope taped to the door. "Ms. Thompson" was carefully printed on it in block letters.

Shauna took it down and tore the envelope open. She pulled out a sheet of paper and stared at it stony-faced for a few moments, then passed it to me.

It was a laser-printed sheet that read:

Ms. Thompson is my own true lady
Though she is dark and kind of shady.
She will return my love, I hope,
My Nubian princess, my Ethiope.

I was uncomfortable being a witness to this torment. "Well, it's sort of a love note, I guess," I said, trying to be soothing.

"And sort of racist, and sort of funny, and sort of ignorant. My people come from West Africa, not Ethiopia." Her voice was shaking with anger, though she hadn't raised her voice.

"Definitely all those things," I said. "But clearly the work of an adolescent boy."

"Or someone trying to sound like an adolescent boy?"

"Well, yes, that could be too, I suppose. It would have to be someone who knew terms like 'Nubian princess' and 'Ethiope.' A well-read adolescent boy?"

We were still standing in the hallway outside the door to Shauna's classroom. The bell had rung and the halls were filling with students.

"We'd better go inside," Shauna said. Her hand shook a little as she put the key in the door and opened it.

We entered and were quickly followed in by two of Shauna's seniors, a boy and a girl.

"Hi Ms. Thompson," said the boy, a freckle-faced

redhead. "Gonna read Chaucer for us today?"

"Sure, Hayden. I wouldn't want to disappoint you," she replied, recovering her poise with amazing speed.

I admired her resilience, but I wondered how many years of adjusting to slurs and insults it took to acquire that kind of poise. Or maybe some people were just born that way.

Students quickly took their seats and chattered noisily until Shauna spoke.

"Okay, folks, we read 'The Wife of Bath's Tale' last night, right? Let's look at the Prologue first. I'll start us off."

Pages rustled as students found their place in the book.

"Experience," read Shauna, "though noon auctori-tee

Were in this world, is right ynogh for me

To speke of wo that is in mariage;

For, lordynges, sith I twelve yeer was of age,

Thonked be God that is eterne on lyve,

Housbondes at chirche dore I have had five."

From my seat in the back of the room, I could hear the students murmuring to each other as she finished.

"Isn't she great?" asked one.

"I love it when she reads that stuff."

"I get it all but the 'lordynges,'" declared a dark-haired girl near the front. "What's that?"

"Think of it as 'masters' or just as a polite form of address," Shauna replied. "So what is she saying, Alyssa?"

"She's saying that, speaking from experience, marriage is full of woe, and she should know because she's had five husbands, starting when she was twelve," the girl answered. "I can't imagine being married at twelve!"

"Wasn't Juliet like twelve or thirteen too?" asked the boy named Hayden. "They did it young in those days."

"Yes, they did. Five husbands! Did she love them all?" asked Shauna. "Megan?"

"Sort of," answered a petite blonde seated at the back of the room. "She really loved the one who beat her. That's twisted. The ones who were older, though, she could control them."

"But what's all that about Venus and Mars?" asked a boy in a Yankees cap.

"Read it for us, Gabe," Shauna suggested.

He gave her a sheepish grin then proceeded to read,

"For certes, I am al venerien
In feelynge, and myn herte is marcien.
Venus me yaf my lust, my likerousnesse,
And mars yaf me my sturdy hardynesse."

"Translation?" Shauna asked.

"She gets her feelings, like lust, from Venus, and her heart — or is it hardiness? — from Mars," said Gabe.

"It's both. 'Heart' and 'hardiness' were similar ideas

back then. So she's lusty like a woman and sturdy like a man," said Shauna. "Remember what we said about the signs for male and female being from the signs for Mars and Venus? So what do you all think of the Wife of Bath so far?"

"She's kinda cool," said one girl, smiling appreciatively. "She got rich from all those husbands, and now she can do whatever she likes."

"I think she's an early feminist," Hayden said. "She wants to be in control of men."

"That's not what feminism is!" protested Alyssa.

* * * * *

Class went by quickly. As the hour came to an end, Shauna summarized what they had discussed. "Now for tonight," she said, "I want you to consider the story she tells. How likely is it that her story is true? That is, given her age at marriage and the ages of her husbands, who would you expect to rule the house and who would control sexuality? Would she have any reason to falsify the tale of her youth? Write down your thoughts and be ready to read to the class what you've written tomorrow."

After the students were gone, Shauna asked me to stay for lunch.

"Sure," I said. "Is there a group of people you usually have lunch with?"

"Jonah and the history posse," she replied as she

locked the door to her room. "On Thursdays we all have the same lunch period."

We headed down to the lounge. On the stairs, Shauna stopped suddenly and turned to me.

"Did you say something about Jonah writing lesson plans in verse?" she asked.

"Yup, iambic pentameter, in fact. I think he was an English major for a while before he switched to history. Wait — you don't think he wrote that note?"

"Well, I hope not, but I intend to find out."

As we entered the room, I saw the same group of young faculty gathered around the table, eating salads and sandwiches, and talking loudly. At another table, some older faculty, including Leo Loops, shared a quieter lunch.

Shauna slid down into a chair next to Jonah. She pulled the poem out of her large leather bag and handed it to him without a word.

"What's this?" he asked, glancing quickly at the paper. "A poem? For me?"

We watched him intently. His eyes widened in surprise as he scanned the page. The others at the table were suddenly still, staring at the three of us curiously.

"Geez," Jonah said. "This is pretty weird. One of your students write it?"

"I don't know," said Shauna. "I thought you might have some idea."

"Me? Why?" I could see the light dawn on his

face. "Oh no, you thought I wrote this? Because Dr. Lombardi mentioned that I write poetry? Come on, Shauna, you know me better than that. I would never...."

He seemed genuinely hurt — or else he was a very good actor.

"What's this all about?" Marianna asked. Shauna passed her the poem. She read it quickly and looked up, her dark eyes gazing sympathetically at Shauna. "That's a fifteen-year-old boy with a crush," she said. "He thinks he's being complimentary, not insulting."

The poem made it all around the table in a few minutes, and everyone concurred with Marianna's assessment.

"Okay, I'm sorry, Jonah," Shauna conceded. "I just thought you might be playing some sort of misguided prank."

"I wouldn't do that," said Jonah. Then he smiled. "And if I were going to write you a love poem, you can be sure the meter would be a whole lot better."

CHAPTER SIX

I pulled my car right up to the curb in front of Buonarotti's, surprised to find a space there. Then I saw Elaine standing in front of the restaurant, a puzzled expression on her face.

"It's closed!" she called.

"No, that's not possible," I said, getting out of the car.

Together we stared at the sign. COMING SOON, it read, JUAN O'HERLIHY'S IRISH CANTINA.

"But Buonarotti's was here just two weeks ago!" Elaine said. "And they didn't mention anything to us about its closing."

"Maybe the waiters didn't get any notice," I replied. "I've read about things like that in the papers. The staff show up for work one day and find a sign on the door, and they're out of work."

"Well, now what?"

"We could try that Chinese place down the street," I suggested.

"You mean Lotus Blossom?"

"Mm-hmm. Swash and I have been there, and it

was pretty good."

"Okay, I'll meet you there."

She eased her tall, lithe body into her Acura and drove away. I followed her the three blocks to Lotus Blossom. We were greeted at the door by the smiling owner, who seemed to recognize me, though Swash and I had eaten there only a few times. He showed us to a corner booth and handed us each a menu.

"Nice-looking place," murmured Elaine as she sipped her water. "It's very peaceful with all these pale neutral colors and the sound of the fountain."

"The General Tso's is very good here," I said. "Chicken or shrimp."

"Mmm. But I was so looking forward to pasta tonight." She frowned at the menu.

"Maybe lo mein will satisfy that craving?" I said.

In the opposite corner of the room, a young man sat down at a grand piano.

"Piano player at a Chinese restaurant?"

"It's the owner's son," I replied. "I thought he only played here on Saturday night."

"Well, he's massacring the Mozart," said Elaine. "I think I need a drink. Is there a wine list?"

"It's in the back of the menu," I said, hoping she would find something she liked. I needn't have worried. Soon we were both sipping a good fumé blanc and munching huge crispy noodles.

"So — have you seen Shauna?" Elaine asked after

we had given the smiling waiter our order.

"Mm-hmm. I was at Hilliard High just last Thursday."

"How's she doing?"

"As a teacher, fine," I said. "She knows her stuff, and she knows how to communicate with adolescents. They think she's cool."

"She always was her own toughest critic," said Elaine. "So what do you think about her so-called problem?"

"I think it's got to be difficult being the only African-American teacher at a lily-white school," I replied. "And someone is playing mean pranks on her to capitalize on her discomfort." I explained about the books and the note.

"Shauna mentioned the upside-down books when she phoned to ask about calling you, but now this poem! She must be feeling just miserable. Even Wintonbury — with all its social snobbery — had a large enough contingent of black students so that no one was really an outsider."

"And of course, at Yale she had plenty of African-American classmates. But I think Shauna's holding her own. And she knew when she took the job that she'd be in the minority. It's mostly the pranks that are getting to her."

"Will you be able to help her figure out who's responsible?"

The waiter arrived with our hot and sour soups before I could answer.

My eyes watering after the first spoonful, I answered, "Well, I'm going to try. I'd really like to see her succeed at Hilliard."

Elaine coughed. "Potent soup!" she said. "Delicious though." She took a big gulp of her water.

"So what's the latest news in your corner of the world?" I asked.

"I'm putting on *Antigone* this fall," she replied. "Always a good one for a girls' school. And I'm thinking of *Chicago* for the spring musical."

"An interesting choice of heroines," I said. "Martyrs and murderesses."

Elaine gave me her biggest smile. "Give 'em the old razzle dazzle," she sang softly.

"And speaking of razzle dazzle, what's up with the elusive Jon Henninger?"

"Ah, Jon! He's not so elusive. He was up for the weekend." She closed her eyes and enjoyed the memory.

Jon was Elaine's on-again-off-again lover, a writer of juicy exposés of the rich and famous. I'd finally met him a few months before and found him charming, handsome and evasive. He was currently living in Manhattan and, according to Elaine, writing a novel dedicated to her.

"And how's his novel coming?" I asked, as the entrees arrived.

"I didn't ask. I don't want to pressure him."

There was a long pause as I tried to think of an appropriately cynical response.

"This lo mein is pretty good, by the way," she said, filling in the silence.

"Mmm. You have to taste my Dragon and Phoenix too," I said. "It's perfect." I put a sampling of chicken and shrimp on her plate. "You know, Elaine, I think you should do *Antony and Cleopatra* instead of *Antigone*."

"Hmm. I've never directed that play. Are there enough female roles? And what made you think of it? Does Jon remind you of — oh, you're making fun of me, aren't you?"

"Yes," I said. "As I've told you before, when it comes to Jon Henninger, you're the Queen of Denial."

CHAPTER SEVEN

"Very funny, Susan," Elaine said, downing a lo mein noodle with a most unladylike slurp. "But I really do think he is writing that novel. You just need to get to know him a little better."

"Mmm," I said, hoping she would take that as agreement.

"I've got a fabulous idea! Jon is coming up from New York again this weekend. Why don't you and Swash join us for dinner on Saturday? I'll cook something special for that gourmet husband of yours."

"Swash and Jon? That would be an interesting evening! I really don't think he'd...."

"Well, you've often said that Swash needs to get out more, and here I am offering you the perfect opportunity. Why not ask him tonight?"

Reluctantly, I agreed. We finished our food and sat sipping our tea.

"Back to Shauna," I said. "Do you know any of the faculty at Hilliard High? It would be good if there were someone at the school who could mentor Shauna."

"I know the drama teacher, of course, and the chair

of the English department is the wife of one of Warren's partners, so I used to know her socially."

Warren was Elaine's ex, an attorney who had left her for one of the younger associates at his firm. She seldom mentioned him, but from her days as the wife of one of the Hartford's most prominent lawyers, Elaine still had a social network that encompassed most of Who's Who in central Connecticut.

"Amelia Rafferty? You know her? Is she a good person — someone Shauna could trust?"

Elaine hesitated. "I'd like to say yes," she said finally. "But she was one of those people who pretty much dropped me when Warren and I got divorced, so I don't know about trust. I think as a professional, though, she'd be helpful to someone who had Shauna's promise as a teacher."

"Well, that's good to know, I guess. Anyone else?"

"Let me think." She broke open a fortune cookie. "Look at this: 'Good news is on its way.' Ah, that must mean Jon is calling tonight. Maybe he'll have heard from his agent about an advance for the book."

"You were thinking about Hilliard," I prodded.

"Oh yes. Hmm." She chomped down on the cookie and then sipped some more tea "I know! Little Leo Loops!"

"You know Leo Loops?" I asked in wonder. "And you call him *Little* Leo?"

"Yes, Leo and I went to the same dancing school

when we were children. His parents were very old money and just the sort of people my mother cultivated."

"Little Leo," I chuckled.

"Well, I guess he's not so little now. I was a few years younger, but in grade school, I was also a whole lot taller than he was, so I remember hating to dance with him. And he's always been Little Leo to me since then."

"So is he still someone you know? Have you seen him recently?"

"Not for a few years. When I was in high school, he went off to Princeton, which, of course, made him very glamorous to me. After that, we lost touch for a long while. But when I came back from New York to marry Warren, Leo had married Louise Renfrew, who had also gone to dancing school with us, and so we all kind of picked up our friendship."

"Leo and Louise Loops?" I said, still amused at Elaine's reminiscences.

"Louise is a very nice woman," Elaine replied. "She's also from an old Hilliard family. Their son, Tim, went to Exeter with our Robby."

"And what about Leo?"

"He's a little strange, I guess. He never lived up to his parents' expectations. Leo was supposed to become a lawyer or a stockbroker — never a teacher, and certainly not in a public school."

"Not even a public school in Hilliard?" I asked.

Elaine shook her head. "Not even Hilliard. He's always fancied himself a writer, I think — brilliantly talented but undiscovered — and since he really didn't have to earn a living, he just took up teaching. Later on, he inherited the family mansion, and he and Louise have lived there ever since, rattling around in their twenty rooms."

"So not the person to mentor our Shauna," I concluded.

"Definitely not," Elaine said. "Now about next time? Let's find a new Italian place. The lo mein was good, but it's just not the same as pasta primavera."

The pianist chose this moment to break into a syrupy rendition of "My Favorite Things" from *The Sound of Music.*

"I think we could improve on the ambience too," I said.

CHAPTER EIGHT

Ambience was not the issue when I told Swash about Elaine's invitation to dine with Jon Henninger.

Looking up from the novel he was reading in bed, he sighed. "Why would I want to have dinner with that con man?"

"But you like Elaine!" I replied.

"All the more reason not to encourage her relationship with this guy," he argued.

"Do you think that your refusing to meet him will discourage her? It will just make her defend him all the more."

Swash was about to come back with some devastatingly logical remark, I'm sure, when the phone on my night table rang. I picked it up on the first ring.

"Dr. Lombardi? It's Shauna. Sorry to be calling so late. I tried earlier, but your husband said you'd be out till nine-thirty or so." She sounded calm, but there was a sense of urgency in her voice.

"Oh that's okay, Shauna. You're not interrupting anything important." I looked at Swash and smiled sweetly. "Did something else happen at Hilliard?"

"Yeah. I got another little present today. Probably from that same inept poet. Can we meet somewhere tomorrow after school? I don't want you to have to drive all the way to Hilliard."

I thought for a moment. "Tomorrow's Wednesday, which means I have a four o'clock class. Could you come to my office? Say, three or three-fifteen?"

"Sure. I could do that. School ends at two, so I could easily make it."

"Do you know how to get to Metropolitan?" I asked.

"I've got a general idea. I'll get specific directions from Jonah."

"That'll be good. But before you hang up, won't you tell me what the present was?"

"I think I'd rather have you see it," she answered. "You'll be amused, I promise. See you then, Dr. Lombardi!"

"Now whatever can that be?" I said, replacing the phone in its cradle. I repeated the conversation to Swash.

"Now I'm curious too," he said.

"You? You're never curious," I replied. "You don't even want to meet Elaine's mystery man."

"Actually, I was thinking about that as you were talking to Shauna. Maybe I will go. But only if you let me drive my new car...."

"The Bel Air? Why not? It'll look perfect in

Elaine's driveway, right next to her Acura and Jon's silver Audi."

* * * * *

Shauna bustled into my office right at three. I was willing to bet she had turned some heads on the way from the visitors' parking lot to the education building. She was wearing a long black jersey dress and platform shoes. A multi-tiered silver necklace glistened on her chest and long silver earrings dangled almost to her shoulders.

"Sorry about the getup," she said. "I've got a dinner date in New Haven, so I changed at school and came straight here."

"Lucky man," I said.

"Yeah," she agreed with a radiant smile. "He was the TA in my lit crit class last year. He's still a grad student at Yale and I've gone out with him a few times. Nothing serious though."

"Did Jonah get to see you looking like this?"

"Jonah? No, he missed the fashion show. But he's just a friend," she said. "And he swears he didn't write the poem."

"Speaking of which, what do you have to show me?" I asked.

"This," she said, drawing something out of her black leather handbag.

It was a large manila envelope, marked 'For Interdepartmental Mail.' Written on it in the same block letters that had been on the poem were the words, "FOR THE DIVINE MS. T."

I peered inside. It appeared to contain a large quantity of coins of some sort. I looked at Shauna.

"Dump them out on your desk," she said.

I followed instructions and found my desk covered with New York City subway tokens.

CHAPTER NINE

"Tokens. Get it?" Shauna said, her eyes fiery with anger.

"Oh! You mean...?"

"Yeah, like I'm the token black person at Hilliard, right? Funny, isn't it?"

"No," I said. "Not funny really. But someone went to a lot of trouble to do this."

"What do you mean?"

"Well, you know the subways use cards now. They stopped using tokens in 2003. You can't get these any-more." I looked more closely at the metal discs on my desk, then laid them out in two rows. "Some of these look pretty old. I bet you can get them on eBay or a similar site, if you're willing to spend the money."

"So what does that tell us?" she asked, half to her-self.

"Well, your prankster poet has gone to some effort and expense to get these. He or she knows about websites like eBay and was familiar enough with New York City to know they had subway tokens a few years ago."

"That could be almost any student at Hilliard High," she said. "They're all rich and spend a lot of time online. Lots of them go to New York on weekends to see Broadway shows and shop on Fifth Avenue."

"Could be some of the faculty too, I guess."

"The richer ones maybe. Definitely not Jonah or any of the younger faculty. They wouldn't waste money on something like this."

"So we're no further ahead in discovering who it is," I said with a sigh.

"Not unless you want to dust them for finger-prints," Shauna said.

"I'm glad you're keeping your sense of humor about this."

"Sometimes I get furious about it," she admitted. "But tonight I'm looking forward to a great dinner at Zinc and a jazz concert, so I can look on the bright side."

"Let's think about this some more," I suggested. "First it was the books and then the poem, and now this. The person responsible knew enough to distin-guish black authors from white ones."

"That's not so hard."

"Oh, I don't know," I said. "I've had history majors in my class who thought Harriet Beecher Stowe was African-American. Prank number one shows at least some familiarity with books and writers."

"Okay, I agree. And the poem, bad as it was,

showed some sophistication too, didn't it?"

"Mm-hmm. Terms like 'Ethiope' and 'Nubian' aren't in the ordinary fifteen-year-old's vocabulary. And now the subway tokens."

Shauna glared. "So you think it's one of the faculty?"

"Well, as you said, one of the richer faculty." I thought immediately of what Elaine had said about Leo Loops and his inherited money. "I suppose it could also be a very well-read senior."

"We do have a few who are amazingly avid readers," she said. "But what do you think I should I do?"

"I'm not sure," I said. "None of these pranks are really harmful, just mean-spirited and annoying. Talk to your friends about the pranks and see what they think. You're pretty sure it's not any of them. And maybe you should tell your department chair."

"Amelia? Why?"

"Elaine Dodgson says that she knows Amelia and that she's a good person. As an older faculty member, maybe she'll have some insight into the situation that you and your friends don't have."

Shauna got up to go. "Thanks, Dr. Lombardi. I'll take your advice. I'll talk to her tomorrow."

We shook hands, and I watched her stride down the hallway. I hoped she'd have a great time with her grad student and forget her troubles. I also hoped the pranks, if they continued, would remain harmless.

* * * * *

"Subway tokens?" asked Swash. "They've sure got creative pranksters at Hilliard High. Whatever happened to leaving frogs in teachers' desk drawers?"

"Well, I guess Hilliard's youth is just a bit more sophisticated than you and your classmates in Hewlett were," I said, naming Swash's hometown in suburban Long Island.

"Maybe," he replied. "Or maybe the prankster world has more resources now, what with the Internet and all." He turned back to his computer. "Let's see what we can find on eBay."

A few taps on the keys and a couple of clicks later, he had found what he wanted. "Here we are! 'Twenty-five classic small Y cutout tokens in use from 1953 to 1970,'" he read. "Twenty-five dollars for the batch with eleven dollars shipping."

"That's a lot for shipping. I wouldn't think they were that heavy."

"Yeah, we can do better. How's thirty Y tokens for thirty-five dollars with only two dollars for mailing?"

"Well, more tokens for the money, I guess, but about the same price. So somebody thought this prank was worth about thirty-five dollars. An expensive prank."

"Not if you have a lot to spend," Swash countered. "Look, you can get a set of custom-made earrings and a charm bracelet made out of subway tokens too."

"Somehow, I think Shauna wouldn't want those," I replied. "And sweetie, I know my birthday's coming up, but don't get any ideas, okay?"

CHAPTER TEN

"Swash, this car is huge!" I said as I slid into the passenger seat of the Chevy for the first time. "I can't remember when I last sat in a car this size."

"Isn't it great?" he said, beaming at me. "I bet your dad had something this big in the fifties."

"Of course he did. One of those Chryslers with the tail fins that made it look like it was about to fly. He kept it well into the sixties, and hated to part with it. But these days, it just seems so excessive."

"Listen to that engine," he continued.

"Mmm," I said.

I decided I might as well just enjoy the ride and the stares of the pedestrians as Swash piloted his treasure down Main Street in Wintonbury. It didn't take long before we were pulling into Elaine's driveway. She'd moved her car into the garage, but Jon's silver Audi with its New York plates was already parked to one side of the driveway, leaving lots of room for Swash's car.

"What a beauty!" exclaimed Jon, rushing out the front door and striding down the drive to greet us.

Swash got out and ran his hand lovingly over the

hood. "Thanks. She is gorgeous, isn't she?"

"She sure is. So you're Swash. Elaine's told me so much about you, but she forgot to mention your exquisite taste in cars. Hi Susan, good to see you again. Swash has good taste in women too."

I could tell that Jon was turning on all of his charm, and he had a lot of it. That steel gray hair, perfectly coiffed, those light blue eyes fringed with long black lashes, a strong straight nose and just the suggestion of a dimple in his chin. *Too handsome*, I thought, not for the first time. And then the casual but expensive clothes, all cashmere and khaki, and the gracious manner that put everyone right at ease. It was all too too much, but Swash seemed to be buying it.

Elaine appeared at the door just as I arrived at her front stoop. "Come on in, you guys," she called. "It's too windy to stay out there, and I've got hot hors d'oeuvres."

Jon looked disappointed but dutifully complied with her request. Swash followed him inside.

"I've got Kir," said Elaine. "And Jon is drinking martinis. There's ale and stout too. What can I get you?"

"Stout for me," Swash answered.

"Kir's great," I said.

"So how well do you know Bel Airs?" Swash asked Jon as Elaine disappeared into the kitchen.

"The '57 is a classic," replied Jon. "Does she have the fuel-injected two-eighty-three?"

"She sure does," Swash said, grinning from ear to ear.

"Wow. Those are hard to come by. I'm impressed."

"First American engine to get one horsepower per cubic inch," added Swash proudly.

"Yeah, that was some engine," Jon agreed. "You know, most people think fuel injection was an invention of the eighties, when emission standards got stricter, but they forget about the Bel Air. So it's not a frame-off?"

"Nope. Almost all original parts. The upholstery's been redone though."

"Sweet. And what a design. I love that ribbed rear panel."

I decided it was time to find out what Elaine was up to in the kitchen.

* * * * *

"How are the men getting along?" she asked, as she loaded hot crab puffs onto a teak tray.

"Too well," I said. "Did you know Jon was an expert on classic cars?"

"Oh, is he?" She smiled what I can only describe as a goofy grin. "He never fails to amaze me."

"Did you mention to Jon that Swash had bought a '57 Chevy? I could swear he's researched it."

"Hmm. I can't remember now. I might have said something...."

We moved back toward the living room, where I

could hear the words "anodized steel" and "V8 engine" being bandied about.

"That's quite enough male bonding," announced Elaine. "Time for the men to abandon all the car talk and entertain their ladies fair."

Rolling my eyes, I handed Swash his stout. I deposited my Kir on the coffee table and plopped down on the couch beside him.

"So, Jon, how's your novel coming?"

"Slowly, I'm afraid, Susan. Fiction is a lot harder to write than I'd imagined."

That's funny, I thought to myself, *because half of what you say is probably fictitious.*

"What's your book about?" asked Swash.

"It's part character study, part romantic comedy," he replied.

Elaine sipped her Kir and looked proud.

"I understand from Elaine that the girl sleuth has a new mystery to solve," said Jon, pouring himself another martini.

"Tell them about the tokens," Swash prodded.

Didn't anyone else notice how adeptly Jon had changed the subject?

"Tokens?" echoed Elaine.

I gave in and told Elaine and Jon the story of the subway tokens and what Swash and I had found on eBay.

"Why are they tormenting her like this?" Elaine asked.

"Well, I don't know about torment," I said. "She's taking it all in good humor. But she's angry too."

"Angry? I'd be furious! You have to find the culprit, Susan."

Jon leaned toward me. "Why not set a trap for the evildoer?" he said.

"A trap?" I asked. "What sort of trap?"

"Could you and Shauna hide somewhere in her room and wait for the person to appear?" suggested Elaine.

"No," Jon said. "If they're watching Shauna's room, or if they know her schedule, they'd be looking for Shauna to leave before they did anything. Perhaps Shauna could leave and Susan could hide."

"But that means Susan would have to get into the room without anyone but Shauna knowing she was there," said Elaine. "Could you sneak in through the window?"

"It's on the second floor, Elaine. I think not."

Swash was looking decidedly unhappy about the prospect of any hiding and sneaking activities on my part. "I wish you two wouldn't encourage her," he said.

"Well, I'll just give it some thought," said Jon. "I bet there's a way to find this prankster — without Susan's having to do any second story work."

"Jon will come up with something," Elaine said. "He's very devious."

CHAPTER ELEVEN

"Jon's an interesting guy," said Swash as we got back in the Bel Air at the end of the evening.

"Interesting? To say the least." I sighed.

"What?"

"Don't you see how smart he is? Elaine must have told him about your new car, and suddenly he's an expert on Chevy Bel Airs! What better way to win you over?"

"Oh, come on! You don't think he learned all that just to impress me?"

"Yes, I do. Jon is the consummate con man."

"But why? Why would he want to con *me*?"

"I don't know," I was forced to admit. "Maybe he just wants you to like him so you'll give your seal of approval to his dating Elaine."

"As if she cares."

"Well, it can't hurt if Elaine's friends like him. And besides, you've got money. Just wait till he proposes some great venture that needs a little of your capital."

Swash shrugged. "That's not going to happen. Let's just say it was an enjoyable evening and agree to disagree about Jon, okay?"

"Sure." After decades of marriage, I knew that sometimes this was the best policy. But I couldn't shake off the uncomfortable feeling that I was getting to like Jon too.

* * * * *

I arranged to meet with Shauna and Amelia Rafferty the following Thursday after school. That gave Shauna time to consult with Amelia about her problem before I got there, and, I hoped, time to come up with a plan to expose the prankster as well. Perhaps my services as a hider-and-sneaker wouldn't be needed.

It was starting to rain as I pulled into the Hilliard High lot. I parked between two BMWs, both so highly waxed and polished that they seemed to deflect the enormous droplets of September rain onto lower status cars like mine.

When I got to Shauna's classroom, she was sitting at her desk talking to an older woman who I assumed was Amelia. Sensible, short white-blond hair and wire-rimmed glasses gave her a properly academic look, while her tanned, muscular body told of a summer spent on tennis courts or golf links — probably both. She and Shauna looked up and smiled as I entered.

"Hi, I'm Susan," I said, putting out my hand. "You must be Amelia."

"Good to meet you," she said, giving my hand a

firm grasp. "I'm glad you advised Shauna to come to me. This is a shameful thing that is happening."

"I agree," I said, pulling up a chair. "I'm glad you're both here."

"What can we do?" asked Shauna. "There's been nothing new this week, but I don't think the pranks are going to end unless we find the person responsible."

"Well, I'm not sure what to do yet," I said. "Amelia, do you think there's any point in letting others know what's been going on?"

"No, not yet," she replied. "We certainly don't want to get that incompetent idiot who calls himself a principal involved in this. He'll only make an announcement at faculty meeting and embarrass everyone."

"How about setting some sort of trap for the prankster?" I suggested.

"Like what?" Shauna's eyes lit up at the thought of hatching a plan to ensnare the culprit.

"I don't know exactly. Do you think that he — or she, though it certainly seems like a he — watches your classroom? So that he knows when you're here and when you're not?"

"It does seem that way. But maybe he just knows my schedule. In a small school like this, everybody knows where everyone else is supposed to be."

"But don't you spend your free period in the classroom on some days and go to the faculty lounge on other days?" asked Amelia. "Are you predictable?"

Shauna thought about this for a moment. "I guess I am pretty much a creature of habit."

"So if you stayed in your classroom a few times when you usually go to the faculty lounge, might that catch the person unaware?" I said.

"Maybe," said Shauna. "But only if I stayed out of sight. It's pretty easy to see me through the glass in the door when I'm at my desk."

"Well then, how about taking a chair into that far corner by the storage closet where you couldn't be seen from the hallway?" Amelia suggested, pointing to the corner.

"Okay, I might try that for a few days," Shauna agreed.

"Good," said Amelia. "Let's try that first, before we start assuming the culprit is somehow doing surveillance on your classroom."

"Thanks, Amelia, I'll start tomorrow. Now you better look into that other mystery."

"I'll do that," Amelia said. "Good to have met you, Susan. Sorry to be rushing off."

After she had left, I turned to Shauna. "What other mystery?"

"Oh, it's Leo Loops. Remember that weird guy in my department? He didn't come to work today. He never misses work, even when he's sick. And he didn't call in. Amelia's phoned his home twice and gotten no answer, so she's pretty concerned."

"Hmm. That *is* strange. I hope it's nothing serious."

Shauna gave a little wave of her hand to indicate that she wasn't worried.

"So, are you ready to spend some time hiding in this room?" I asked.

She gave me a dubious look. "I suppose I can do without my friends in the history department for a few days," she said.

We chatted for a few minutes more about how her classes were going. As I got up to leave, Amelia came hurrying into the room.

"I can't get my car started," she explained. "I wanted to stop off at Leo's house on my way home and see what's going on, but now I can't start the damn car, and I've got to call Triple-A and wait for them to come."

"What's the problem?" asked Shauna. "Maybe we could help, and then you wouldn't have to wait around. Do you need a jump?"

"No, I don't think we can fix this ourselves. It just makes a grinding noise when I turn the key. I've had this happen before — something gets loose, I think. I told Bob that I need to get a new car, but we keep putting it off. And I'm so worried about Leo."

"Where do you live?" I asked. "Maybe I could give you a lift home."

"On the south end of Hilliard," she said. "About ten minutes from here. And Leo is just a few blocks away. If you could do that, I'd be very grateful. Then Bob and I could deal with my car and Triple-A when he gets home."

"Oh, that's perfect," I said. "I live in Wintonbury so you're right on my way. I'd be glad to take you to Leo's and then home."

Bidding Shauna goodbye, Amelia and I trekked to my car and set off. I was happy to help and also eager to satisfy my curiosity about the legendary Leo Loops.

CHAPTER TWELVE

"Turn right at the next corner," said Amelia abruptly. We'd begun the ride by discussing Shauna's problem, but soon I found myself extolling Shauna's performances in WAG's drama program.

I saw a sign for Buttonwood Way and turned onto a street of enormous old houses with huge expanses of lawn.

"There," she said, pointing to the biggest house on the street. "Number six. You can pull into the driveway and I'll run in."

I did as I was told and sat admiring the beautiful stonework of the Loops's house as Amelia hurried down the flagstone path to the front door. She returned about two minutes later.

"No one home," she said. "I rang and rang. Then I used the brass door knocker. I'm really worried. Could Leo be in the hospital? Why wouldn't Louise have called and told the school secretary?"

"Did you try the door?" I asked.

"It was locked."

"Is there a back door?"

"I didn't think to try the back door," she said. She gave me a conspiratorial look. "Should we do that? Or maybe talk to a neighbor? Or call the police?"

"I don't think we should bring in the police," I said. "But maybe Leo and his wife are sick or injured in some way. Let's try the back door, and if that isn't open, perhaps one of the next door neighbors has a key for emergencies."

"All right, let's do it," said Amelia.

We ran across the soggy lawn to the back of the house. Sure enough, there was a back door, and it was unlocked.

The door opened into a spacious kitchen. I stood at the threshold dripping rainwater on the floor, but Amelia immediately started calling "Leo! Louise!" and running from room to room through the house. There was no answer to her calls.

Having convinced myself that this wasn't really breaking and entering, I decided to look upstairs. No one was there. As I headed back down to the kitchen, I heard Amelia shouting from somewhere below.

"What is it?" I yelled.

Amelia appeared at a door just outside the kitchen. Her face was ashen. "Down in the basement," she said, gesturing toward the stairway behind her. "It's Louise. And I think she's dead. Call 911."

I had no desire to see for myself. Finding one dead body was my personal quota, I felt, and I had achieved that a year earlier. So I picked up the phone that hung from the kitchen wall and dialed. But then I realized that I didn't have firsthand information to give the person at the other end and quickly handed off the phone to Amelia.

"It's six Buttonwood Way," I heard her say. "The owner, Louise Loops, is lying at the bottom of the basement stairs and I think she may be dead. There's blood around her head, so she may have fallen and hit her head. I can't rouse her and I can't find a pulse. Please send someone at once. Six Buttonwood Way."

Amelia hung up the phone and sat down heavily on a kitchen chair. "Oh Susan, I'm sorry you got dragged into this. You don't even know Louise or Leo."

"I'm glad you weren't alone when you found her," I said.

"Me too." She shuddered. "Thank you."

"Don't thank me. If I hadn't encouraged you to break in, you might not have found the body at all."

"All the more reason to be grateful. She might have been lying there for days if we hadn't let ourselves in. Where in hell is Leo? I've know him for twenty years and he's never — oh where is that ambulance?"

She looked so distraught that I was afraid she was about to faint. I asked her if she'd like a glass of water.

"No, that's all right," she said. "Just let me sit here."

I went to watch out a front window while Amelia remained in her chair. Within a short time, a firetruck, an ambulance and two police cars pulled up in front of the Loops's house. I opened the front door to admit two police officers and three EMTs and pointed them toward the kitchen. Curious neighbors stood outside gawking while Louise's body, covered with a sheet, was brought out the back door to the ambulance and carried away.

A young policewoman, whose nameplate identified her as Officer Archambault, came out of the kitchen a few minutes later. She was blond and attractive in a no-nonsense, no-makeup way.

"And you ma'am," she began. "Are you a friend of the deceased too?"

Ma'am? Was I that old?

"No, I don't know the Loopses, at all," I said. "I was just giving Ms. Rafferty a ride home, and she asked to stop here so she could check on the Loopses. Mr. Loops hadn't made it to school today."

"Yes?"

"So when no one answered, Ms. Rafferty was really worried. I suggested we try the back door, and it was open. And then when she went down the basement to look, she found the body."

"So you have no idea where Mr. Loops could be?"

"None. In fact, I've never actually met him. I did *see* him once in the hallway of Hilliard High."

"Okay. Give Officer Murphy your name, address and phone number, then you're free to leave."

I went up to the young policeman who was jotting

down Amelia's information and supplied mine. Then, with simultaneous sighs of relief, Amelia and I left the house and climbed back in my car.

Soon we were at the Raffertys' more modest home a few blocks away.

"Goodbye, Susan," Amelia said as she hopped out of my car. "I'll see you soon, I'm sure. We'll take care of Shauna's problem. And thanks again for the lift. I'm so glad you were there when I found Louise."

"Me too," I said and waved goodbye. *Finding a body together can be quite a bonding experience*, I thought.

* * * * *

For the next few days, every newspaper in the Hartford area was full of the Loopses: Louise's death and Leo's disappearance. All the articles referred to Leo as the "scion of a prominent Hilliard family." It reminded me of the coverage of the Wintonbury Academy murder; the newspapers used the phrase "the elite Wintonbury Academy for Girls" so much that we thought of calling the school EWAG afterward.

There were Leo Loops sightings everywhere. Witnesses were sure they saw him shopping for almonds at Trader Joe's in West Hartford, buying gas at the Fast-Mart in East Hartford, and attending a rock concert in Middletown. The only place he wasn't seen was in his classroom at Hilliard High.

CHAPTER THIRTEEN

"Little Leo Loops a murderer?" said Elaine. "Don't make me laugh!" And then she did — a light silvery laugh that made some of the other patrons of Juan O'Herlihy's Irish Cantina turn to stare at the source.

Rather than scouting for a new Italian restaurant, we had decided to swallow our pride and try out the eatery that had usurped the spot of our beloved Buonarottis's. So far, we had eaten our fill of corn chips and salsa and were sipping sangria and waiting for our entrees.

"But Elaine, what else would explain his disappearance and her death?"

"Maybe the Mafia was after them both," she answered. "They got Louise, and now Leo's in hiding."

"Does Little Leo being in trouble with the Mafia sound any more likely to you than his being a murderer?"

"No, I guess not," she admitted. "Maybe Leo left — ran off with another woman — and Louise threw herself down the stairs in an attempt at suicide?"

"A successful attempt," I added. "We're not even

sure if Louise was killed by the fall, or killed by someone else and then thrown down the stairs."

"I know," she said. "The newspapers have been very hush-hush about the whole thing. What do you think?"

"Elaine, I have no idea. I never really met Leo — I just walked past him in the hallway my first day at Hilliard. I don't have any idea what he's capable of. And as for Louise...." I shuddered as I remembered seeing her body carried out to the ambulance.

"Well, I can't really say I know much about Leo these days either. It's been years since I saw him. I wonder where he could be hiding."

"Does he have relatives anywhere nearby?" I asked.

"He and his son are the last of the Hilliard Loopses," she replied. "I think maybe there's a branch of the Loops family down in Greenwich or New Canaan. But wouldn't relatives be the first people the police would contact?"

"I guess so. What about his son?"

"Tim? I think he's in New York i-banking."

"Just like Joanne," I said, with a sigh.

"And my Robby. What is it with i-banking?"

"The money, obviously. Our children are half our age and making twice our salaries."

Elaine was nodding her agreement just as our paella arrived. Conversation halted for a while as we sampled the cuisine.

"Mmm, great sausage," I said, my tongue tingling from the spices.

"I think the mussels are a bit off though," said Elaine, wrinkling her nose.

"Eww, you're right. Okay, let's skip the mussels."

"Where were we?" she asked.

"Leo. If *you* were Leo where would you hide?"

"That's a tough one. If I were *me* — which I am — I'd hide out at Jon's apartment in Manhattan. You and Swash are the only ones who know about Jon, and you'd never give me away."

"You mean you haven't told your kids yet?"

"I don't need any more disapproval, thanks," she said. "I have yours."

"Oh Elaine, I...."

"Though you do like him just a little bit better since our dinner, don't you, Susan? I know he and Swash really hit it off."

Before I could formulate my answer, a pair of strolling guitar players began to sing — loudly.

"Saved by the mariachi?" asked Elaine with a wry grin.

"What about mariachi? I can't hear you too well."

"I said, 'saved by the mariachi?'"

"Oh, *si*," I said, returning her smile. "Yes, I am beginning to like Jon better. I just don't trust him yet. It's going to take a while before I do."

"Well, he'll be around for a long while, so take your time."

At this point, we were both shouting over the din of the music, so we turned our attention back to our paella. Now and then, we tried a little stab at conversation, but we soon realized that having a substantive discussion would be impossible.

Then, strumming 'Donkey Serenade,' the musicians made their way to our table.

"Request, senorita?" one asked.

"Senorita, ha!" chuckled Elaine.

I smiled and shook my head, hoping they would go away. Instead, they started a raucous version of 'South of the Border,' which the younger of the two seemed to be directing at Elaine. We waited them out, smiles frozen on our faces, until the song ended and they headed across the room to a middle-aged couple.

"Whew!" I said. "Thank goodness that's over. It sounds a lot better when Sinatra sings it."

"Let's ask for the bill and get out of here," Elaine suggested. "I can do without dessert."

I nodded and we called the waiter over.

"Back to Leo," I said while we waited for the bill. "Any guesses as to where he would go?"

"I seem to remember a house Leo and Louise used to have at the Vineyard. Maybe he's hiding there."

"Would the police know about that?"

"Maybe not," she replied. "Is it my civic duty to

inform them about the house, do you think?"

"I don't know. If you feel strongly that Leo didn't kill Louise, maybe you should just keep out of it. Let the police work things out without your help."

"That's just what I'm going to do. After all, I haven't seen him in years. I'm sure Amelia has told them about the house on the Vineyard by now."

"Unless she's protecting him," I said.

We paid the bill, left a tip, grabbed our jackets and headed for the door. The musicians had just begun a rousing rendition of 'Danny Boy.'

"Let's try a different place next time," I called as Elaine waved goodbye.

CHAPTER FOURTEEN

The following day was a frustrating one at Metropolitan. Nanette, my department chair, was trying to set up the class schedule for the spring semester. I usually helped plan the schedule for the secondary education courses, so I was accustomed to the chaos involved, but somehow this time was worse than ever.

"Dammit!" she said. "The physics department went and scheduled their methods course for Mondays and Wednesdays at two. They said they wouldn't do that again."

"Typical," I replied. "They should know that's when science majors are supposed to be taking the ed psych course. Well, maybe we can move the ed psych to Tuesday and Thursday. Oh no, that wouldn't work for the bio majors."

"How about if the science majors took ed psych with the English and history majors on Monday and Wednesday mornings?"

"Yeah, we could do that. We just need to put in an extra section. Let's see. Okay, that works." I looked at the clock. "Can we continue this tomorrow, Nanette? I have to get ready for a class."

She shrugged. "Sure, I'll go back to the elementary ed courses. They're a mess too."

My class was not very lively that afternoon. The heat of an unexpected Indian summer seemed to make everyone listless and uninspired. After practically turning cartwheels to get some interest in the discussion, I let the class out five minutes early and drove home.

The house smelled of peanuts and cilantro, so I knew the minute I entered that Thai was on the menu for that night. Swash was in the kitchen, stirring the sauce and singing along with Ella Fitzgerald. It was Cole Porter's "You'd Be So Nice To Come Home To."

"Good choice," I said, giving his cheek a kiss. "It *is* good to be home."

"Hard day?" he asked. He looked sympathetically at me but didn't wait for an answer. "I've had an interesting day myself."

"Tell me about it. My day isn't worth talking about."

"Well — fanfare please — I joined the Metropolitan Classic Car Club today."

"Metropolitan? You mean there's a classic car club at my university?"

"Indeed, there is. It meets once a week on Thursday nights. I'm not surprised that you haven't heard about it. They seem to keep a low profile."

"But why did you join a car club? I thought you

were doing a lot of that Chevy Bel Air stuff online."

"Let's talk over dinner. Go change out of those professor clothes."

I pulled on a pair of jeans and a T-shirt and returned to find the table set and a heaping bowl of pad thai waiting for me.

"Okay," I said, after a few ambrosial mouthfuls and some appreciative murmurs. "Now tell me about this momentous decision."

"Well, I think the simple answer is I'm bored staying home all the time."

"Really? But what about your hedge funds? Your IPOs?"

"I'm still going to do all that. It doesn't take much time anymore." He saw my questioning look and grinned at me. "Yes, I'll still do the cooking too."

"Whew, I'm glad to hear that." I looked at the rapidly dwindling pile of peanuts and noodles and thought of how little I knew about preparing a meal as good as this one.

"I'll just be out on Thursday nights. And maybe I'll go to a few car shows."

"Car shows too?"

"Yup." Swash sipped his tea and then added, "You know the online stuff doesn't seem to cut it in this case. I think I need to kick a few tires."

"I can understand that. Well, I'm glad you're going to do it. I bet you'll have a fine time. And I think it's great that you're going to get out more."

"Yeah," he agreed. "I have become something of a recluse over the years."

"Not that you were ever a big party guy."

"What? We had some big-time parties when we were in grad school!"

"Swash, Renaissance fairs don't count as parties."

"When your field is Renaissance Studies with a philosophy minor, they have to count. And besides, we always drank a lot of wine."

* * * * *

"So how was it?" I asked, looking up from the book I was reading in bed when Swash returned from Metropolitan the following night.

"It was kind of fun," he replied. "Of course I'm the oldest one there, but no one seemed to care."

"What did you do?"

"Well, as a newcomer, I had to introduce myself and describe my 'ride.'"

"Your what?"

"My ride. You know, the Bel Air. Then I had to talk about how I got into cars in the first place."

"Weren't you nervous?"

"No," he said. "I enjoyed talking about myself, actually. And the guys seemed to enjoy listening, though I think they had trouble believing I was old enough to remember when Bel Airs were new."

"And after that?"

"Oh, we spent a lot of time on planning the fall car show — that's in late October — and then some people told stories about their cars and about drag racing and stuff like that."

"Drag racing?"

"Don't worry. I'm not going to do that. But I am excited about the car show. Will you come?"

"I wouldn't miss it," I said. And I meant it.

If this was to be Swash's version of a midlife crisis, so be it. Elaine's ex-husband Warren came to mind. *Better old cars than young women*, I thought.

CHAPTER FIFTEEN

We expect each student to become an
effective communicator who expresses ideas
clearly through various means to
a variety of audiences.

— from the Mission Statement of
Hilliard High School

A week had gone by since Amelia and I had found Louise's body. Although I followed the Leo Loops case in the local newspaper, I tried to curb my curiosity until the date that Shauna and I had previously arranged for me to return to visit her classes.

I couldn't see anyone in Shauna's classroom when I arrived, though the school secretary had assured me she was there. I knocked loudly on the door and Shauna appeared from the far corner that she and Amelia had chosen as her hiding place.

"Enter the inner sanctum," she whispered as she let me in. "No one in here but us hermits."

"Has it been that bad?" I asked.

"Worse. I haven't left this classroom during a free period all week, and I've got Jonah watching it while I eat lunch."

"At least you're not skipping lunch."

She gave me a wry smile. "Lunch isn't much fun without Jonah."

"Aha!" I said. "Is that a hint of romance I hear?"

"Just good friends, same as ever," she replied with a shrug. "I've got the Yale TA for romance, remember?"

"Mm-hmm. How could I not remember the Yale TA? So the phantom prankster hasn't been seen?"

"Nope. But it's been pretty lively here anyway. Here, come look at this." She indicated the computer at the front of the room and pulled up two chairs.

"This is about Leo's disappearance, I assume." I took a seat and looked at the screen.

"Yeah, this is the unofficial Hilliard faculty bulletin board. It's like a faculty chat room. Leo's all anyone can talk about."

Shauna clicked on an icon of a blackboard, and a list of messages appeared under the heading *Where's Leo?*

Okay, guys, who's taking bets on Leo's being found by the Hilliard police department?
— Geologyrocks25

They're not gonna find him. He's in Tahiti by now!
— Dreamsofsummer

With a South Seas sweetie on each arm.
— Purrkitty

You people are disgusting. His wife is dead, and maybe he's injured and lying in a ditch some- where. Have some compassion!
— JaneAusten2000

I agree. You've already convicted him of Louise's murder. Innocent until proven guilty, remember?
— Herstory93

He sure murdered my interest in English when I was a student here.
— Geologyrocks25

I think he's hiding nearby and will turn himself in soon. Then, when he gets enough publicity, he'll get a big book deal. He's always wanted to be a published writer, remember?
— DiamondLily

"Wow! There's not a lot of support from his col- leagues, is there?" I said. "I'm amazed that the admin- istration lets you put all this stuff online."

"Only a few administrators even know about it, and they turn a blind eye. A teacher set it up as an in-house board. No one outside the faculty can read it, so we can post anything we want. It goes on for pages like that. And if you think that's bad, you should hear what the students are saying!"

"Do I want to?"

"Well, the students' bulletin board gets cleaned up every hour by the administration, so that's not much fun to look at, but Gabe — you saw him in my Chaucer class — has a blog that's pretty good." Shauna clicked again and brought up another page on the screen. "Here's what he's saying about Leo."

I'm pretty sure I saw Loopy in the Stop & Shop on Mulberry Road yesterday. He was wearing a black bushy beard and California shades, but I could tell it was him. I think he's going to spend his declining years as the Robin Hood of Hilliard. There sure are lots of rich people to steal from but where, oh where, will he find any poor to give to?

"Another sighting," I said. "How many of those do you hear about every day?"

"About a dozen," she sighed. "It's a quiet day so far."

"So life at Hilliard High is otherwise normal?"

"Pretty much. But enough playtime," she said,

standing up. "I've got to get ready for my next class."

"What are you planning to do?"

"Well, I've had them read the first half of *Pudd'n-head Wilson* this week. Today's our first discussion of it."

"*Pudd'nhead Wilson?*" I said. "I don't think I've ever heard of a high school class reading that. That's pretty daring of you!"

"It was actually Amelia's idea. It's on the optional list of readings for the juniors — they do American Lit and the seniors do Brit Lit. Amelia thought that if I wasn't too uncomfortable doing it, it would bring up the issue of race that's underlying all the pranks."

"And maybe someone will come forward with some information you can use?"

"Or reveal himself unintentionally. In any case, it's clearly on their minds, so why not deal with it, she said. And I agreed." She picked up a paperback edition of the book. "I hope this works."

CHAPTER SIXTEEN

We expect each student to become a
collaborative learner who understands his/her
own position as well as the multiple
perspectives of others, and actively participates
in classroom discourse.

— from the Mission Statement of
Hilliard High School

The class filed in, chattering noisily. I recognized most of them from my first visit to Hilliard High, although there was one blond girl who seemed unfamiliar. She wore black jeans with a black jacket, both heavily decorated with metal loops, studs, and zippers. Her eyes were darkened with black liner. *Hilliard's only Goth*, I thought to myself, looking at the others in their brightly colored T-shirts and khakis.

"So," began Shauna, "you were supposed to read

the first hundred pages of *Puddn'head Wilson* this week. Did everyone get that far?"

"I finished it!" said a boy in a striped shirt.

"Me too!" said a girl with a dark auburn ponytail.

"Wow," Shauna said. "Anyone else besides Zach and Jenna finish it?"

Hands went up all over the class.

"Okay, let me ask it this way: Did anyone *not* finish it? It's okay to say so — I only assigned the first hundred pages."

Not one hand was raised.

"Well then, I guess we don't have to worry about spoiling the ending for anyone. That actually makes it easier for us to talk about it. Now why did everyone keep reading?"

I saw students looking around at one another, reluctant to answer.

"Jenna?" Shauna prompted.

The girl's face reddened. "I — I couldn't believe you assigned it," she said. "It was full of the — the N-word!"

"Yes, it was," agreed Shauna. "But is that why you kept reading?"

"No," Jenna replied. "It was a good story and I wanted to find out what happened to the two boys who were switched."

"It's kind of a murder mystery," said Zach.

"Yeah, I liked that he used fingerprints to solve it,"

added another boy.

"I like that too, Dave," Shauna said. "It was one of the first uses of fingerprints to solve a crime, in a book at least. Twain wrote it in 1894."

"No CSI back then, huh?" he replied with a broad smile.

"Nope. But let's talk about the two boys, Tom and Chambers. What about them? Brittany?" Shauna nodded at a tall brunette in the back of the room.

"Well, one was white and the other was — well, he wasn't black exactly — he couldn't have been because they looked so much alike. But he was a slave, so...." Brittany pulled at her bangs in confusion.

"But he was one thirty-second black," Zach said. "So that made him black according to the law."

"So was he white or was he black?" asked a boy who hadn't spoken before. I remembered him as the distracted one in the class I'd seen a week or two earlier. He wasn't distracted now; the whole class was riveted by this topic. "He was white enough for Roxana to switch their identities."

"Good, Travis," said Shauna. "It's a book about identity, isn't it? So what constitutes identity?" She paused. When no one answered, she continued, "Is it race? Is it how we're raised? How society treats us? Or is it simply a matter of our fingerprints?"

"I—I don't know," Travis replied. "I think Twain thinks it's how we're raised. I think Tom, who's really

Chambers, turns out bad because he's spoiled and pampered so much by Roxana."

"And Chambers, who's really Tom?" asked Shauna.

"He can't live in the white man's world at the end, even though he's white, because he's been raised as a slave. So I think that Twain is saying it's all how we're raised."

"But couldn't you say that Twain made Chambers good 'cause he was all white? And he made Tom turn out so bad because he's part black?" argued Zach. "So he's kind of tainted?"

Jenna, who was seated next to Zach, gave him a horrified look.

"No offense, Ms. Thompson," he added quickly. "I'm just saying that Twain might have thought so."

"No way!" said Jenna. "Mark Twain was a good guy. He couldn't have been such a racist."

"But don't 'good' people sometimes have 'bad' ideas?" asked Shauna, putting finger quotes around the words. "If you lived in a time when everyone was racist or sexist, couldn't you be a good person and still have what *we* might think of as bad ideas? Kathryn?"

"An artist or writer should be ahead of his time," answered the girl in the Goth outfit. "Or her time."

"Everyone is a product of the time and place they live in," Brittany said. "Even artists and writers. Even you, Kathryn."

"Okay," said Shauna. "That puts us back to my

question about identity. What makes you *you*, Travis? Is it that you're white? That you're male? That you grew up in Hilliard?"

"It's your DNA," Dave called out. "In Twain's time, they didn't know about DNA so they used fingerprints."

"I'm me because of how I think," said Travis. "And the things I decide to do. It has nothing to do with being white or being from Hilliard or having a Y chromosome."

"So who I am has nothing to do with my being black or female or being from New Jersey?" Shauna countered.

There was an uncomfortable silence. Shauna waited for a while, then turned to a boy who was staring down at his notebook. "What do you think, Jeff?"

I watched as Jeff's face slowly lit up with a smile. "I didn't know you were from New Jersey, Ms. T," he said. "My dad's from New Jersey too. Where'd you grow up?"

"New Brunswick," she replied. "But does that answer the —"

"What did your parents do?" asked Zach.

"Don't ask her that!" said Jenna.

"It's okay, Jenna. My mom was a third grade teacher and my dad was a security guard at Rutgers University. I didn't grow up in the 'hood, if that's what you want to know."

"Did you play sports in high school?" asked Jeff.

Now it was Shauna's turn to smile. "I went to high school right here in Connecticut, at Wintonbury Academy. And I did play basketball for them." She paused. "So now that you know where I grew up, what my parents did, where I went to high school and what sport I played, do you know who I am? Jeff?"

Jeff gave a little shrug as he realized that his diversionary tactics hadn't worked. "Maybe. At least I know *something* about who you are."

"I still think Travis is right," said Kathryn the Goth girl. "What makes you *you* is how you think, not where you come from or who your parents are."

"But how you think is affected by where you live and who your parents are!" insisted Brittany. "That's Twain's point!"

"No, it isn't!"

"Yes, it is!"

CHAPTER SEVENTEEN

"Wow! That was some amazing class!" I said after the students had left the room.

"Yeah, they're an impressive group."

"Well, yes, they are," I replied. "But I meant your handling of all that."

Shauna beamed at me. "Thanks, Dr. Lombardi. I really loved doing it. Oh, here's Jonah."

"Hi, Dr. Lombardi, how are you?" said Jonah, sticking his head into the classroom. "Time for you to go to lunch, Shauna."

"Hey, Jonah, come with us. You don't have to watch my classroom." She took out her keys and locked the door behind us. Jonah gave her a dubious look, but she put her arm through his and led him away. "I don't want to worry about the prankster today. I want to celebrate. Let's all go to lunch together."

At lunch, Shauna and I recounted the events of the last class to Jonah and the history crew. Shauna (unconsciously, I think) imitated the Hilliard accent as she repeated the students' comments.

"So now they're all grappling with who *they* are,

and whether their genes and environment determine their identity," I said. "It was a great class."

"Is that why you're here today, Dr. Lombardi?" asked Marianna. "To observe Shauna's class?"

"No, she's here to catch the phantom prankster," Jonah said.

"I thought you'd be more interested in catching Leo Loops," said Georgia with a wink. "Didn't Shauna say you'd helped solve the Wintonbury murder?"

I couldn't resist. "Actually, Jonah is right. But I am interested in Leo Loops too. Any of you have a theory as to where Mr. Loops is?"

Brett grinned. "Everyone has a theory. Mine is that he killed his wife and fled the country. Loopy had all that family money stashed away in a shoebox, and he used it to get out before the police found the body."

"Amelia found the body," Shauna reminded them. "With Dr. Lombardi."

"I just can't believe that of Loopy," said Marianna, shaking her head so emphatically that her dark curls danced. "Why would he kill Louise? They seemed like such a happy couple."

"Maybe he just needed to break free of all that domesticity," Georgia said. "He felt he was getting old and this was his last chance to find some adventure."

"Adventure?" scoffed Jonah. "Loopy? What do you think he's doing — sailing the seven seas as a pirate?"

"What do *you* think then?" she challenged.

"I think he just lost it. He bashed his wife on the head and ran away. He's hiding at a relative's house, or maybe in the Hilliard Forest."

"Now you sound like Gabe Naughton," said Shauna. "His blog is still comparing Loopy to Robin Hood."

"Fascinating theories," I said. "So he's either Robin Hood or Captain Hook?"

"Or he's nuts," added Jonah.

"Or someone else killed Louise, and Loopy's on the run," Marianna said.

"On the run from whom?" asked Brett. "And why?"

"From whoever the murderer is. I don't know. I just don't think he killed her."

"Marianna believes in love and marriage," Georgia explained. "Maybe that's why she's engaged and we're not."

"What's your theory, Dr. Lombardi?" asked Jonah.

"I don't have one. I never really met either of the Loopses. Does anyone know what Amelia thinks? She was the closest to them, wasn't she?"

"Yeah," said Shauna. "She was. But I haven't had the nerve to ask her — she's been so upset all week."

"She did come up with the *Pudd'nhead* idea for you though," I said.

"Yeah, that's true. But I think the police have questioned her a couple of times, and it's getting to her."

"Hmmm. Well, it seems to me that she's the one whose theory I'd like to hear. Any chance, Shauna?"

"She might talk to you. After all, you were there when she found Louise."

"Maybe I can see her after classes," I said. "I could start by talking about the prankster and then mention something about our finding the body...."

"What about the prankster? Anything new there?" asked Brett.

"Nope," Shauna said. "He's been pretty quiet lately. Maybe because I don't ever leave the room. Speaking of which, I'd better get back."

"Good to see you all," I said, getting up. "Let me know if you have any new theories."

"Hope you find the prankster," said Jonah. "Or Loopy."

"What's next period?" I asked, as we threw away our trash and headed out of the faculty lounge. "More Chaucer?"

"Actually, we're getting ready to write a paper on ol' Geoffrey, so it's a pre-writing class. Nothing too arcane."

"Well, I'd still like to see it," I answered. "And I want to see what's become of your classroom in our absence."

"You don't think the phantom has struck again? We've only been gone about thirty minutes!"

We arrived at Shauna's classroom and she un-locked the door. "Everything looks normal," she began.

And then we saw her desk. The papers and books had been moved to one side, and in the center of the desk was a chessboard. The board was strewn with white pawns, all lying on their sides. In the center stood the Black Queen.

CHAPTER EIGHTEEN

"I can't believe this!" she said. "The first time I leave my classroom unguarded in over a week, and he gets in and pulls off another prank!"

"I think this settles it," I replied. "Someone is definitely keeping your room under surveillance."

"But how?"

Before I had time to think of an answer, Shauna's students started to pour into the classroom. I watched her put on a smiling face and greet them. The class started as if nothing had happened, though a few students near the front couldn't help gawking at the chessboard on her desk. Without interrupting the ongoing discussion, Shauna moved to the desk, casually knocked over the queen, and covered the chessboard with a pile of papers. *What a pro*, I thought.

I sat at the back of the classroom, my thoughts occupied with the prankster and his surveillance. How was he doing it? Could the classroom be bugged?

From my seat, I started to scan the walls. Colorful posters of *Shakespeare in Love*, a recent version of *Othello*, and last year's *Pride and Prejudice* decorated one white wall. On the other side of the room, portraits of women writers, arranged chronologically from Jane Austen to Maya Angelou, gazed down from above a row of computers. The back wall was taken up with a set of bookshelves, all the books inside it now standing right side up. On the whiteboard in front, Shauna was using a bright red marker to record the students' suggestions about possible topics for their Chaucer papers. I couldn't see any evidence of an electronic device of any sort. But it would be small, I thought. And if it were white it might be near-invisible.

The students continued to call out ideas, which Shauna jotted down until the board was full. The class was a lively one, but I was having trouble sitting still. What was that gray smudge near the *Pride and Prejudice* poster? I yearned to get out of my seat and start searching the walls with a magnifying glass, which of course I didn't have. Could I use my reading glasses as a substitute? I looked up impatiently at the clock. Then I saw a little black knob peeping out of a corner of the ceiling near the front of the room. Could it be a camera? I spent the next ten minutes studying the rest of the ceiling tiles.

Finally, the class ended. When the last lingering student had received an answer to her question about "The Pardoner's Tale," I hurried up to Shauna.

"Look up there," I said, pointing to the corner of the ceiling. "What is that?"

"I don't know," she said. "Let's take a closer peek." Shauna dragged a chair over to the corner and climbed onto it. Peering closely at the device, she said, "Well, it's plastic and it looks like it has a lens. It could be a camera, I guess, but it's so small." She pulled at it gently.

"Does it come out?" I asked.

"I'm afraid to pull too hard — maybe it's supposed to be there. I better ask someone. I'll go get Amelia. She should be in her office about this time, I think." She hopped off the chair and headed out of the room.

I climbed up and tried to see if it was a camera. I was almost a foot shorter than Shauna, so I couldn't quite reach it, but I thought I could see a lens peeping out of the device.

Amelia bustled into the room with Shauna behind her as I was clambering down.

"Hi Susan," she said, taking my place on the chair. "Sure looks like a camera of some kind to me too. I can't imagine who could have done such a thing."

"The administration doesn't routinely videotape new teachers, I suppose," I said.

"Covertly? I should hope not," she replied. "If they're doing anything like that, it's a matter for the teachers' union."

"So should we take the camera down then?" Shauna asked.

"Maybe we could just cover its lens but leave it in place," I suggested. "We might want to examine how it's connected at a later date. Or show it to someone else."

"Good idea," agreed Amelia. "Have you any black construction paper handy, Shauna?"

"No," Shauna said. "Do you have some in your office?"

"Top left-hand drawer of my desk. Get some tape from my desk too if you don't have any here."

"I've got tape," said Shauna as she hurried out of the room.

"I just can't believe this," muttered Amelia, still standing on the chair.

"It seems like a lot of strange things are happening at Hilliard High these days," I said, craning my head so I could see her face. She looked drawn and tired.

"Yes," she said. "The whole Loops affair is really wearing me down."

"I was hoping to talk to you about that some more, if you wouldn't mind, Amelia."

"I'd like that. After I get back down to the floor again. And after we take care of Shauna's little problem."

Shauna returned with the black paper and handed it up to Amelia with a roll of tape.

"You're taller than I am, Shauna," Amelia said after a moment of consideration. "You can probably do a better job. Just wrap the paper around the camera and tape it on."

Shauna and Amelia switched places while I stood by, feeling useless.

"Before you wrap it up, see if can you find anything printed on the plastic," I said.

"Okay," Shauna replied. "Here's some writing. Looks like it says mini-something. 'Mini-watch,' that's what it says. Then 'wireless.' Damn, it really is a camera, isn't it?"

"It certainly sounds like it," I said. "Let me see if I can find something like it online."

While Shauna finished covering the lens with construction paper, Amelia and I went to one of the computers and searched online for a 'mini-watch.' Several sites came up immediately, and I clicked on one called 'Smarthomeware.com.'

"There it is!" cried Amelia triumphantly.

"Yes, and it's on sale," I said. "Only ninety dollars."

CHAPTER NINETEEN

"This month's hot deal," read Shauna, as she came up behind us. "Mini-Watch wireless color cam. Easy to set up and use." She sighed. "Great."

"It comes with a receiver," I said, pointing at the picture on the screen. "And according to this, the receiver has to be less than a hundred feet away. Should we try to find it?"

"The receiver looks pretty tiny, and it could be a hundred feet in any direction," Shauna objected. "It might be pretty hard to find."

"But it has to be sending the picture to a TV somewhere, doesn't it?" said Amelia. "It's the TV we need to track down."

"A hundred feet," I said. "That's not too far, is it? And since you're in a corner room, that eliminates two directions, right?"

"Well, okay," said Shauna. "Let's go down the hallway in the new wing and see if there's anyplace within a hundred feet that someone could hide a TV screen. Then we can do the same in the old wing."

The hallways were deserted by this time. As we

passed the English classroom next to Shauna's, I said, "Does every classroom have its own TV?"

"TV with VCR and DVD player," said Amelia. "But the prankster couldn't use a TV in a classroom, could he? He'd never be sure the classroom would be empty when he needed to get in and do his surveillance."

"Unless he knew exactly when the classroom was in use and when it wasn't," I replied.

"No, even then he couldn't be sure that a teacher might not appropriate the classroom to meet with a student or just to grade papers," said Shauna. "It has to be a TV tucked away somewhere."

We passed Jonah's room and saw him talking to some obviously adoring students. Shauna gave him a little wave and continued walking.

"A fine young man," Amelia said with a smile at Shauna. Then she stopped abruptly in front of a closed door. "Hmm, how about this storeroom? Have you ever been in here, Shauna?"

"No. I don't know whether it belongs to the English department or the history department, as a matter of fact."

"Well, it was ours once, but no one in the English department ever used it, so we gave it to the history folk so they could store their maps and such. Let's see if I still have a key." She took out an enormous brass ring with twenty or more keys attached and looked dubiously at it. "It's hopeless. I can't remember which key it is, or if I gave it back. I'll just call Silas. Be right back."

"Silas is our custodian," explained Shauna as Amelia scurried back to her office. "Nice guy."

"Let's see if there are other locked rooms on this hallway while we're waiting," I suggested.

"I think there's only a closet where Silas keeps his stuff, down at the other end," she said.

We walked a little farther down the hall and it appeared that Shauna was correct: there was nothing but more classrooms and a closet. By the time we were back to the storeroom, Amelia had returned and a large man with a salt and pepper beard and a long gray pony-tail was coming toward us.

An aging hippy, I thought. Then I chided myself: if he's aging what does that make me? I smiled as Amelia introduced me and he nodded in return.

"So you ladies want to get into the storeroom, huh? Sure, my master key can open it up for you."

He put a key in the lock and opened the door. "Just slam it shut when you're done. I'll be right down the hall."

He sauntered away, leaving us alone. After a few minutes of searching, it became obvious that there couldn't be a TV hidden among the maps and books stacked in no discernible order in the storeroom.

"Do you think it might be in Silas's closet?" I whispered.

"Why Susan, you distrust everyone, don't you?" asked Amelia.

"Well, you never know," I said. "Couldn't we get a peek into his closet?"

"Sure," agreed Shauna. "We could just go thank him for his help and get a quick look."

With Amelia still frowning, we headed down the hallway. Shauna knocked on the closet door, which was slightly ajar, and then opened it wide enough for all of us to see inside.

Silas looked surprised to see us. For a moment as he gazed at me, I thought there was something familiar about him. I tried to mentally remove the beard and see his features, but no one specific came to mind. I reassured myself that he was just a vague replica of all the modernist English professors at Metropolitan.

"Silas, could we borrow your master key for about twenty minutes?" Amelia asked, trying to cover her embarrassment.

"Sure, Ms. Rafferty," he answered. "Looking for something special? Maybe I can help you."

"No, that's okay. It's just something that's gone missing from the English department office and I wondered if it had wandered down the hall somewhere." That sounded pretty flimsy, even to me, but Silas didn't question her further. I had the feeling that no one questioned Amelia very often.

With Silas's key in hand, she led us back past the

English classrooms and into the old wing. We explored every closet and storeroom on that hallway and then did the same on the first floor. The master key didn't work on the administrators' offices but we did get into the science and art storerooms and the closet where the band uniforms were kept. There was no sign of a hidden TV.

"It wouldn't be in the principal's office or the guidance wing, anyway," said Amelia.

"Unless the principal is spying on new teachers now," I said.

"Susan, Mr. Richardson may be an idiot at times, but he's not unscrupulous," Amelia replied. "And he certainly doesn't have time to come up with these pranks, even if he were smart enough."

CHAPTER TWENTY

Amelia turned to Shauna. "I don't think we're going to find it," she said. "At least not today. But we've taken care of the problem for now. The Phantom won't be spying on you through that lens for a while." She patted her on the back. "Go home and get some work done. Or go to the gym. Forget the pranks for a while."

"Thanks, Amelia. I'll try," Shauna said. "Thanks, Susan. I think it was fantastic how you spotted that damn camera." She hurried back to her classroom and emerged a minute later with her bookbag. Waving good-bye, she disappeared down a stairway.

"So, can you give me a few minutes to talk about Leo?" I asked.

"As I promised," said Amelia, ushering me into her office.

I took a seat. "What's happening?"

"Well, that Officer Archambault has been here to question me twice so far. I think she's suspicious of me because I'm a friend of Leo's."

"You don't actually know where he is, I suppose."

"Of course not!" She looked at me with disappointment. "If I knew, don't you think I'd tell the police? I don't think Leo did it, but I was Louise's friend too, and if she was murdered, I want them to catch the killer."

"If? You still think it may have been an accident?"

"Honestly, I don't know what to think. That Archambault person keeps asking me about their marriage and whether they argued a lot. How would I know? Does anyone ever know what really goes on in someone else's marriage? They never fought in public, I can tell you that."

"And the rest of the Loops family? What are they doing?"

"Well, the medical examiner finally released Louise's body, and Tim, their son, had her buried. There was a private funeral for family and a few friends. Bob and I went, of course. It was terribly sad."

"I can imagine," I said. "Poor Tim. What a terrible burden for a young man to have to carry. His mother dead, his father missing, and not knowing if his father is a murderer."

"Did you know Tim?" she asked, brightening a little.

"No, but I did hear about him from Elaine. Elaine Dodgson."

"Is she a friend of yours? I remember Shauna mentioning you had taught at Wintonbury."

"Yes, she's a dear friend."

"Well, next time you see her, give her my regards.

We, uh, kind of lost touch over the years."

"I will," I said, not sure how Elaine would react. Elaine has been known to hold a grudge for decades.

"You know, I've thought about calling Elaine dozens of times. I still feel bad about not seeing her after the divorce."

Why is she confiding in me, I wondered. Maybe finding a body together was even more of a bonding experience than I had realized.

"About Leo? You don't *know* where he is, but do you have any theories?"

"I've thought and thought. Bob and I have discussed it every night at dinner, and, of course, everyone I know has called to ask me what I think."

"And what have you come up with?"

She sighed. "Nothing. It's all so out of the realm of normal experience, isn't it?"

"Yes," I agreed. "But if you *had* to make an educated guess?"

She leaned toward me. "Well, I'd never say this to the police, but I'd guess that Leo is nearby."

"Why? What makes you feel that way?"

"Leo is Hilliard, Hilliard is Leo. He's always lived here. No one knows this town and all its ins and outs like Leo. If there are hiding places in Hilliard, Leo knows about them."

"Hiding places? Like what?"

"Well, you know Hilliard was on the Underground

Railroad back before the Civil War, right?"

"I guess so. Lots of these little Connecticut towns were."

"And the Loops family was very well known for its abolitionist activity."

"So you think that he...."

"If I had to look for Leo — which I am not about to do, by the way — I would look in some of Hilliard's oldest houses. I'd look for little rooms hidden behind staircases and closets." She gave me a conspiratorial smile. "And that's my educated guess."

"But someone would have to be providing him with food and water," I said. "Who could be trusted to do that?"

"I haven't a clue. It's just a theory after all. I haven't worked out all the details."

"Wow, that's quite an ingenious theory, Amelia." I looked at my watch. "I've got to go, but if you think of anything more — about Leo or about the Phantom Prankster — let me know. I'll probably be back early next week to help Shauna look for that receiver."

Amelia took my hand. "I'll look forward to that," she said. "You and Shauna do make life at Hilliard High so interesting."

* * * * *

"Underground Railroad?" said Swash as he tossed the salad. "Fugitive slaves? Wow."

"My word exactly. Wow. Isn't that a great theory?"

"Yes, very clever. But she's not going to the police with it?"

"Nope," I said, spearing a piece of grilled salmon with my fork. "I think she's very conflicted about whether she should be helping Leo or helping the police catch him."

"And you?"

"Me? I know you're going to find it hard to believe, Swash, but I'm staying out of this one."

He picked up his glass of sauvignon blanc. "I'll believe it when I see it," he said.

CHAPTER TWENTY-ONE

My resolution to stay uninvolved in the Leo Loops disappearance lasted all through Friday night and into the first part of Saturday morning, when I received a phone call from a forlorn Elaine.

"Jon's not coming up this weekend," she said. "I've got no rehearsals scheduled and nothing much else going on."

"This isn't like you," I said. "You're always overwhelmed with things you have to do: board meetings to prepare for, papers to grade, shows at the Hartford Stage."

"I know, I know. I've just gotten too damn dependent on Jon for entertainment. I have to pull myself together." She paused. "So how about some lunch, and maybe a bit of shopping?"

"Absolutely no shopping. Not after what happened last time."

"Last time?"

"You don't remember?"

"Oh, you mean that little raspberry silk dress? It looked so beautiful on you — just fabulous with your dark hair."

"That's what you said when you encouraged me to buy it," I replied. "Which I did. Too bad I have nowhere to wear it. Now it looks just fabulous in my closet."

"Well, what would entice you to do something with me this afternoon?"

I hesitated, looking dubiously at my desk piled high with papers.

"What about something vaguely educational?" Elaine persisted. "A museum?"

Sad to say, that was all the stimulus I needed for my resolve to disappear.

"How about a tour of one of the historic houses of Hilliard?" I asked.

"Leo!" she said. "You're looking for Leo!"

"Yes," I admitted. "It's an idea that Amelia Rafferty put in my head."

"Amelia's very clever," Elaine mused. "I do miss her sometimes. Well, sure, why not? Which house?"

"Which ones do you know? Is there one that has Underground Railroad connections?"

"You want the old Winthrop place. That's on Miller Road, just past Prexy's Café."

"Okay, I know where that is. How about we meet there about noon, take the tour, and then go have some lunch at Prexy's?"

"You're on!" she said, hanging up and leaving me to explain to Swash where and why I was going.

"Try not to get in too much trouble," was all Swash said as I left. His nose was in a book titled *Hot Wheels*.

* * * * *

It was late October, but we were having another of those fine Indian summer days that occasionally bless New England. Elaine was waiting on the steps of the Winthrop House as I pulled into the parking lot. She had on a long skirt printed with amber and rust-colored leaves and a golden suede jacket. I was glad I'd changed out of my jeans and sweatshirt into nice slacks and a navy blazer. I'd never look as glamorous as Elaine, but at least I could be respectable.

As we opened the door, a sixtyish woman in a nineteenth century costume greeted us with a smile. "Oh good! I was afraid that with this beautiful weather, no one would show up today. Welcome to the Josiah Winthrop House."

We were standing in a small foyer. To our left and right were doorways leading to a parlor and a dining room, both elegantly furnished. Directly ahead of us was an ornate grandfather clock and a stairway leading up to a balcony.

"Sign the visitors' book, please," she said, still smiling broadly.

As we signed, she continued, "I'm Mrs. Truesdale, and I'm a volunteer with the Hilliard Historical Society. I'll be giving you your tour."

"What a lovely staircase," said Elaine.

"Yes," our guide agreed. "It's very special. You see how it goes up to a balcony that has a door on either side of it? That balcony is called a 'Good Morning Walk' because it joins the two bedrooms. One can get up in the morning, open the door to the balcony and call a cheery 'Good Morning!' to the person in the other bedroom."

What if you're not exactly cheery in the morning, I wondered.

"Then of course, one would make one's toilette and go down the other stairs to the breakfast room," she said. "But I'll show you that later. Now let's go on to the parlor."

Elaine followed her, murmuring about the moldings. I stifled a yawn and trudged behind them.

"The house was built in 1752," Mrs. Truesdale said. "The furnishings, though, are from the late nineteenth century, which is when the house was last occupied by the Winthrop family. We've done everything we could to reproduce what their home was like then."

As Mrs. Truesdale showed us through room after room, Elaine, who had toured the Winthrop House about a decade earlier, asked questions about wallpaper and furniture. At the third enormous fireplace that we were required to inspect, I could stand it no longer.

"Isn't there some rumor that this house was part of

the Underground Railroad?" I asked.

"It's not a rumor at all," replied Mrs. Truesdale. "It's absolutely true. Here, let me show you."

I winked at Elaine as we followed our guide out of the enormous kitchen and into the pantry.

"See?" she said, pointing to what appeared to be a wall lined with shelves. She pulled on one of the shelves and the wall came out like a door, revealing a small stairway behind it. Carefully we tip-toed down the steep stairs and found ourselves in a small room directly below the pantry.

"This is where the Winthrops hid the runaway slaves," she said proudly. "The Winthrop family were very active in the abolitionist movement, of course."

I looked around. The room was empty except for a few dusty old wooden chairs. There were no signs of any recent habitation.

"Thank you," I said. "It's so interesting to see a bit of history like this."

We went back upstairs. As we passed through the parlor, I noticed a door in the wall.

"Does that lead to the garden?" I asked.

"No, that's the Coffin Door," she replied. "None of the other doors were wide enough for a coffin, so they had to have that one put in special. People died at home in those days, you know."

"And some still do," Elaine replied. "Like Louise Loops."

"Oh, wasn't that awful!" Mrs. Truesdale said, shaking her head. "I do hope they find him. Such an awful thing to have happen here in Hilliard."

CHAPTER TWENTY-TWO

Elaine and I said our goodbyes to Mrs. Truesdale. With the warm sun still overhead, we decided to walk the short distance to the Olde Hilliard Shoppes. It was typical of our luck with restaurants that our old favorite, Prexy's Café, had been miraculously transformed into a coffee emporium called The Hill of Beans. Completely redecorated with posters from *Casablanca*, it seemed to attract a different crowd than Prexy's did, many of them taking advantage of the WiFi access that was available. Taking a quick look at the posted menu, we saw that it was still possible to order the kind of lunch we had in mind, so we took a table in a quiet corner.

"Hi! I'm Kathryn and I'll be your server," said the smiling teenager who quickly greeted us. "Hey, I know you!"

I looked at her more closely. It was Shauna's "suburban Goth" girl. With normal clothing and less eye makeup, she was barely recognizable.

"Oh yes, you're in Ms. Thompson's class. I was in the class when you were all discussing *Puddn'head Wilson*."

"Yeah, wasn't that cool?" she said.

"You like Ms. Thompson, I bet," said Elaine.

"Mm-hmm. She's way more interesting than most of the other teachers at Hilliard." She took out her pad and pencil. "Now what would you ladies like to order?"

"I'll have a Caesar salad and an iced tea," I said.

"Same for me," said Elaine.

"Would you like chicken with that?" Kathryn asked in her most professional manner. "They marinate it in really great spices and then grill it."

"Sure, why not?" Elaine replied.

"That sounds perfect, Kathryn. Make it two."

After she'd left, I explained to Elaine about Kathryn's alter ego. The iced teas came quickly, and we got back to our conversation about the Winthrop House.

"That tour wasn't terribly illuminating," I said.

"You're just disappointed that Leo wasn't waiting for us at the bottom of the stairs. I bet you envisioned him crouching in a corner like a hunted animal."

"I'm sure he's here in Hilliard somewhere," I said.

"There are at least two other historic houses with hidden rooms that I know of," said Elaine. "And maybe some others that aren't open to the public."

"So you think I should just give up on the whole idea of finding Leo?"

"I suppose so." She hesitated, then smiled. "Would I sound too much like Swash if I said that I think you should leave Leo to the police?"

"Yeah, that does sound like Swash," I agreed. "But

this time he's too absorbed in his classic car stuff to worry about me." I sipped my tea and considered Swash's new hobby. "And what's with Jon? Why isn't he up for the weekend?"

"He's in the throes of his novel," she replied. "He says he's going strong right now and didn't want to break the mood. Of course, I miss him, but I didn't want to be responsible for distracting him from his masterpiece."

This was Jon Henninger's first novel. His previous two books had both been bestsellers, but even his agent had been dubious about his ability to write fiction.

"He calls me his muse," Elaine continued. "What kind of muse would I be if I complained when he was working hard?"

I groaned.

"I know you still don't like him, Susan."

"That's the problem," I said. "I *am* starting to like him. I told you that. I just don't think you should believe everything he tells you."

"Well, liking him is half the battle, I guess," said Elaine with a shrug. "Now tell me more about Shauna. Any clues to the prankster?"

"We've got a great clue. I just don't know where it leads."

I told her about the surveillance camera and the unsuccessful search for its receiver. By the time Kathryn delivered our salads, we were deep into Shauna's mystery.

"Well, you've certainly got a sophisticated prank-ster on your hands," Elaine said. "Subway tokens, chess pieces and surveillance cameras."

"Not to mention the poetry and the upside-down books," I added. "Almost too sophisticated to be a student, you think?"

"It couldn't be another faculty member, could it?"

"I suppose it could be another teacher — maybe one who was jealous of her success with the students. But somehow, I don't think so. Some of the pranks seem just too mean for an adult."

"And you think that adolescents are too caught up in their own worlds to notice anyone else's pain? Yes, we've certainly seen many instances of that, haven't we? I suppose you're right." She looked down at her salad. "Mmm, she was right about the spices, wasn't she? Good choice."

We finished our lunch, and leaving a generous tip for Kathryn, we headed to our cars.

"Where shall we meet for dinner next week?" asked Elaine as she unlocked her door.

"Decisions, decisions. It used to be so easy when it was just Buonarroti's. Let me e-mail you about it. I want to find a better restaurant than we've been visiting lately." I waved goodbye and she drove off.

* * * * *

I was nearing the bottom of my stack of papers

when Elaine called again.

"Hi Susan. I just got off the phone with Jon," she began.

"Oh no! Has something happened?" I was worried that Jon had done something despicable.

"No, nothing. He's fine. We're fine. The novel is moving along nicely."

I breathed a sigh of relief. "Then...."

"Why am I calling?"

"Yes. Not that I don't enjoy talking to you, but it's been only a couple of hours since we had lunch."

"It's just that I told Jon about the surveillance camera and he had a suggestion about finding the receiver."

"Ah, his devious mind!"

"Exactly. He said to tell you to think outside of the box."

I sighed in disappointment at the cliché.

"More specifically, he said to think vertically."

"Vertically?" I repeated.

"Yes. He said to look at what's *below* Shauna's classroom. Up to a hundred feet below, in fact."

I thought of that musty basement that Shauna and I had stumbled upon during my first visit to Hilliard High.

"Elaine, of course! Please send Jon my eternal gratitude."

"I'll remind you of that gratitude the next time you besmirch his honor," she replied. "See you next week."

CHAPTER TWENTY-THREE

*We expect each student to become a
self-directed learner who sets priorities, takes
appropriate educational risks, and evaluates
his/her own progress.*

— from the Mission Statement of
Hilliard High School

I phoned Shauna immediately but there was no answer. Out with her Yalie grad student, I thought to myself.

"Shauna, please wait for me after school on Monday," I said to her voicemail.

When I told Swash about Jon's idea, he groaned.

"Now why didn't I think of that?" he asked, looking up from his computer screen. He'd been reading a website about Bel Air collectors. I saw something about a man who owned thirty of them.

"Too busy thinking about your car?"

"Yeah, maybe. I've got to get it ready for the Metropolitan car show in a couple of weeks, remember?"

"I do remember. But I can't imagine what's left to do — it looks beautiful to me."

"Well, I did drive it a couple of times. So now I have to get it detailed again."

"Of course you do," I said. "And I've got to get back to my papers." It was a world I'd never understand.

* * * * *

Monday dawned bright and sunny, one of those crisp autumn days that I love. *Great weather for searching in a dark and dingy basement*, I thought.

I taught my morning class with extra energy, the weather and my own excitement buoying up my spirits. I met with a few students during office hours, read my e-mail, and then set off to my car. I'd driven a few blocks when I remembered that I'd once again neglected to check my voicemail. Damn. I vowed to become more disciplined about voicemail. I'd be sure to check my messages from home this evening.

A sleek black Lexus occupied the space that I'd come to think of as my parking spot at Hilliard High. I didn't care. I just took the next space and hurried to the school entrance. Students were streaming out of the front doors, calling to one another as they headed to the buses or the student parking lot.

The secretary in the main office looked up with a smile. "Ms. Thompson is expecting you, Dr. Lombardi. Go on up."

Shauna was at her desk sorting through some papers when I arrived. "It must be something good," she said, rising from her chair with a grin on her face. "You sounded really excited."

"I didn't want to tell you on voicemail," I said. "I wanted to see your face. Sorry if I left you in suspense."

"That's okay. I didn't get the message till late last night."

Hmmm, I thought, *maybe the Yale affair was starting to heat up.*

"Come on," I said. "We're going to the basement."

Her eyes widened. "The basement! You mean the receiver's in that creepy old dungeon? Why didn't I think of that?"

"That seems to be what everyone says," I replied.

We trekked down to the first floor and over to the stairs leading from the old wing to the basement.

"Wait. Shouldn't we take a flashlight?" she said.

"All set," I replied, pulling two small but powerful flashlights from my leather carryall.

This time the door to the stairs was locked. I groaned in frustration.

"No problem," said Shauna. "I'll just get a set of master keys from the office — or from Silas, if I can't sweet-talk the secretary into giving them to me."

I didn't have to wait long.

"The secretary's a good person," Shauna said, as she unlocked the door. I fumbled for the light switch at the top of the stairs. My fingers finally located it and threw the switch. A light flickered and then with a pop, it went out.

"Damn!" I said. "Wouldn't you know...."

We went carefully down the stairs, shining the lights ahead of us. The smell of mildew and dust became stronger as we descended.

"Whew," I said. "They ought to clean this place out. What a lot of junk." I looked around at the piles of desks and chairs that crowded the vast space.

Shauna was heading toward a corner. "This should be directly below my room," she said, turning her flashlight on the wall. "And what do we have here?"

I rushed over, bumping my shin on an old chair. There was an electrical outlet in the wall and something was plugged into it. We traced the electrical cord from the outlet to one of the desks nearby. On that desk, partly obscured from view by a chair upended on the desktop, was a television. With the illumination from both our flashlights, we could see that there was a small metal box next to the TV. A cable ran from the box to the back of the television.

"Eureka!" I said.

Shauna pushed the power button on the TV. I heard a buzz but the screen was still black.

"Wait here," Shauna said. "I have to go back to my room and take the construction paper off the camera."

I waited. I took a closer look at the TV and receiver. There was nothing especially interesting there except for the name "Mini-watch" emblazoned in red on the metal box. I shone my flashlight around the room. More desks, some old cafeteria tables, a few bookcases, and chairs of all descriptions. Was that a door in the far wall?

A flicker from the TV screen caught my eye, and there was Shauna's face smiling at me. She waved at the camera, and then I watched as she left her classroom.

While awaiting her triumphant return, I investigated the far wall. It was indeed another door, and of course it was locked.

Shauna reappeared while I was still examining the keyhole. "So did you see me?" She looked more closely at the TV screen.

"You came through in all your glory," I said. "But look at this door. Can we try some of the master keys on it?" I asked.

"Well sure, but why? We found what we were looking for. Now we just have to find the person who set it up."

"Person or persons," I corrected her. "And I don't know why — I'm just curious, I guess. I'd like to find out where this door leads."

Shauna shrugged. "Whatever you say." She began

trying the keys on the ring that the secretary had given her. "Here you go," she said after inserting the fourth key. "I'm starting to feel like Alice in Wonderland. I just know there's going to be a little bottle that says 'Drink Me' on a table inside that room."

But the door didn't lead to a room. It opened on another stairway going still further down.

"A sub-basement," I said. "This is some building." I found a switch that operated an overhead light, and treading carefully under its dim illumination, I started down the stairs.

"Yeah, they don't build them like this anymore." Shauna was right behind me. "Oh god, this smells even worse."

She was right. Now I could detect the odor of rotting food in addition to the mold and dust.

"Could this be a place where students hang out?" I asked.

"Students with a lot of master keys? I guess so, but...."

We found ourselves in an almost empty room, smaller than the one above it, and with only one large desk in the center. I shone my flashlight onto the desk. It was littered with greasy papers and bags marked Burger King.

"I think we may have found the secret lair of Leo Loops," I said.

CHAPTER TWENTY-FOUR

"Leo? What makes you think this is Leo's?" Shauna asked.

"Well, for one thing, everyone's been looking for him, right? And Amelia said something about Leo knowing every inch of Hilliard. She was thinking about the historic houses, but it makes sense that he would know about a sub-basement in the high school too. This would be the perfect hideout."

"I don't know. It could be the same student who set up the TV and receiver. We know that he — or she or they — has at least one master key. Why not more?"

"You could be right," I admitted. "On the other hand, we're not sure that he, or she or they, are students, remember? What if it were Leo who was spying on you all along? Shine both flashlights here and let me go through the drawers of the desk. Maybe we'll find something that helps us figure out who's been using it."

I pulled open the top drawer. It contained compartments with paperclips, a stapler, some markers and a calculator.

"This is all very neat," I said. "I can't believe a student would keep it this organized."

There were two deep drawers on the left side of the desk. The top one contained manila folders marked Longfellow, Whitman, Dickinson. Inside were multiple copies of poems by these writers.

"Leo," Shauna said with a sigh. "He's the only other teacher who does American lit."

I opened the second of the drawers. It was filled with paperbacks, their spines upward. Philip Roth, Raymond Chandler, J.D. Salinger, Stephen King.

"Our Leo has quite an eclectic taste for light reading," I said, moving the books onto the floor. At the bottom of the drawer was another manila folder. "What have we got here?"

I pulled out the folder. It was filled with travel brochures. Shauna took them from me.

"Japan, Hong Kong, Thailand," she read as she flipped through them. "And here's Bali — we're getting more exotic."

"Interesting," I said. "You think he's been planning to run away? Oh, look at this!"

It was a page cut from one of those magazines that you find only on airplanes. On the left side was a crossword puzzle, completed in ink. To the right was an ad captioned "Your Japanese destiny awaits."

Focusing our flashlights on the page, we put our heads together and read:

"We are the premier matching service specializing

in introducing professional men in the U.S. to desirable Japanese women. Our experienced counselors work closely with you to help you fulfill your dream."

There were photos of four beautiful Asian women, smiling demurely, and several testimonials from satisfied customers. Robert, age 44, an investment banker, was my instant favorite: "Meeting Yoko was like living a fairy tale. I knew she was a very special lady from day one."

"Ewwww," said Shauna. "Leo was just a dirty old man."

"Maybe not 'just'. He could be a murderer too."

"Let's get out of here," she said, pulling my arm. "I think we need to call the police."

We left the desk as we'd found it, relocked the doors, and hurried up to the main office. As we were about to go in, Shauna stopped.

"Wait. I'm not sure I want the whole school to know that I found Leo's stuff. That's what'll happen if I call the police from the main office."

"I see what you mean," I said. "You'd have to explain what you were doing down there in the basement, and that would mean letting people know about the prankster, wouldn't it?"

She nodded. "So far, only Amelia and the history posse know."

"What did you tell the secretary when you got the keys from her?" I asked.

"I kind of fudged it. I just told her I was locked out of a closet and asked her if she had a *set* of master keys, without being too specific. She probably assumed I meant the English department closet, and I let her assume it."

"Well, I guess the first thing to do is return the set of keys, so she doesn't start to wonder." I looked through the glass door and waved at the smiling secretary. "Then we can go out to the parking lot and call the police on your cell phone."

Shauna went in and returned the keys. Then she ran back to her classroom to get some books and papers while I waited at the front entrance.

"Okay, I'm ready," she said, sounding out of breath. "Now what should I tell them?"

"The truth," I said. "But maybe we should ask to talk to Officer Archambault."

"Who?"

"Oh, I forgot you weren't there. That's the policewoman who interviewed me after Amelia and I found Louise Loops."

"Oh yeah, that was probably her I saw talking with Amelia in the English office a couple of weeks ago. Now let's see — I shouldn't dial 911. I guess I have to call directory assistance and get the main number for the Hilliard police station."

I stood by for moral support as Shauna went through the various channels to get to Officer Archambault. I heard her explain that she'd found something at the high school that might lead to Leo.

"There." She put the phone back in her handbag. "I lucked out. She's on duty today and she said she'd be here in less than five minutes."

The police cruiser pulled right up to the entrance and Officer Archambault got out of the driver's seat.

"You're the person who called?"

Shauna nodded. "Yeah, I'm the one. My name is Shauna Thompson and I teach here."

"Aren't you Dr. Lombardi?" the officer asked, turning to me.

"Yes. Actually Shauna and I were together when we found Mr. Loops's stuff."

"Hmm. You're always right there when people make interesting discoveries, aren't you?"

"Well, I...."

"I left a message for you on your voicemail today. I was wondering when you'd get back to me. I need to ask you some more questions about Amelia Rafferty and the Loops's house. But that can wait. First show me what you two have found."

"Er, you'll have to get a set of master keys from the secretary," said Shauna. "And can you do it without mentioning my name?"

Officer Archambault smiled. "Sure, I can do that. That secretary knows me by now — I've been in and out of here so much lately. I won't even have to explain why I need the keys. Now where should I meet you two?"

Shauna explained where the stairway was, and, skirting the main office, she and I headed there to wait for Officer Archambault.

CHAPTER TWENTY-FIVE

We led Officer Archambault down the stairs to the big storage room and then to the sub-basement.

"How did you find this?" she asked.

"We, uh, were looking for something else," explained Shauna. "Something not related to Mr. Loops."

"Something you don't want to talk about. I see. Well, I'll let that go for now."

"Here's the desk," I said. "We left things just as we found them. But we did look through the drawers, so our fingerprints will be all over them and the papers inside the desk."

"That's okay. It's not a crime scene. You had to look at the stuff to determine whose it was." She pulled open the drawers and rifled through the folders. "Uh, there's nothing here that actually says 'Loops' on it. What makes you think it's his?"

"The folders of poetry," said Shauna. "That's not a student's stuff. And Mr. Loops did specialize in American poets."

"And these travel brochures and the match-making ad? Did he have a special interest in Japan and Thailand?"

"Not that I know of," Shauna replied.

Officer Archambault rubbed her chin. "Well, it *could* be his stuff. But these burger wrappers are a few days old — maybe he's already flown the coop. Or found a new hiding place."

Shauna looked disappointed. "So what will you do about this?" she asked.

"We'll keep a closer watch on the school, especially at night. We have been keeping it under surveillance, you know. If Loops has a master key set, he could well be hiding anywhere in the school, but he might be more likely to come out after dark. You're free to go now, Ms. Thompson. I'm sure it's been a long day. Dr. Lombardi, I'd still like to talk to you."

"Sure," I said. "But please let's all get out of here. The smell is really getting to me. If we need privacy, we can talk in the parking lot — it's pretty empty by now."

When we reached the main hallway, Shauna waved goodbye and headed for the faculty parking lot. Officer Archambault dropped off the keys in the office and then met me at my car as we'd agreed.

"Let's just sit in the car and talk," I suggested. "It's been kind of a long day for me too."

Officer Archambault gave me her quirky smile as she climbed into the passenger seat. "You're not under any suspicion, Dr. Lombardi, so relax. It's just that you turn up at some interesting times and places."

I sighed. "I do seem to have a knack for that."

She got out a small notebook and a pen. "Now let's just talk about Ms. Rafferty. How well do you know her?"

"Hardly at all. It's Shauna I know, and Amelia is her department chair. As I told you when you first interviewed me, I was visiting Shauna here and ended up giving Amelia a ride home because her car was acting up."

"Okay. And whose idea was it to stop at the Loops's house?"

"That was Amelia's idea. Leo had missed school that day and hadn't called in."

"And were you with her when she rang the front doorbell?"

"No," I said. "I was waiting in the car."

"So you don't know that she did ring the bell?"

"Well, she said she did. Why would she lie about that?"

"I don't know." She jotted something in her notebook. "But the point is, you have only her word that she rang the bell. Okay. And whose idea was it to go in the back door?"

"That was definitely my idea. I remember that clearly."

"You weren't at all concerned about entering a stranger's house?"

I thought back. "Well, I did have some misgivings, but Amelia was so worried about Leo and Louise that it kind of overrode my concerns."

"Uh-huh. And when you went in the back door, did you or Amelia call out?"

"Amelia did. As I said, I didn't know the Loopses."

She made some more notes in the book. "Okay, and then you went where?"

"I went upstairs while Amelia went to the basement."

"So you never went to the basement yourself?"

"No," I replied.

"And you never saw the body?"

"No."

"Dr. Lombardi, I'm going to sum this up for you, and you see if I have it right." She looked down at her notes. "You didn't know either Leo or Louise Loops. You drove to their house at the suggestion of Amelia Rafferty. Ms. Rafferty told you that she rang the bell and no one answered. She was very disturbed so you suggested trying the back door. You both entered the house, and you searched the upstairs while she went to the basement. Then she told you she'd found Louise's body, and you called 911. Is that correct?"

"Yes, that's right." I got the feeling there was something I was missing.

"And you know nothing about Ms. Rafferty's relationship to Leo Loops?"

"Well, from Shauna I knew they were longtime colleagues. But as I said, I didn't really know either Amelia or the Loopses personally."

"Okay, Dr. Lombardi, that's all I need. Thank you."
She held my eyes for a moment and then started to slide
out of the passenger seat.

"Wait," I said. "Are you implying that Amelia Rafferty is a suspect in Louise's death?"

"No, I'm not saying that. I just needed to clarify
your relationship to all the parties concerned and to
make sure I had your story correct. Thanks again." She
gave me a goodbye wave as she headed for her cruiser.

As I drove home, I thought about the questions
Officer Archambault had asked. Was it possible that
Amelia had attacked Louise while I was upstairs? I
didn't think so. But what if Louise were hard of hearing
— could Amelia have sneaked up behind her and hit
her with something? Did Amelia have a relationship
with Leo that was more than just collegial? Was she
planning to run off with him to Bali? Then what about
that ad for Japanese women? It all seemed so prepos-
terous.

CHAPTER TWENTY-SIX

The house was filled with the aroma of onions and garlic: Swash's Own pasta sauce. But Swash himself was not in the kitchen. I lifted the pot cover, stirred the sauce and licked the spoon. My mouth still pleasantly hot from the red pepper flakes, I made my way to the garage.

"Hi honey, just letting you know I'm home."

Swash was on his knees polishing the grille of the Bel Air. "It will be a while till dinner," he said. "The sauce has to simmer another thirty minutes. Why don't you change, read your mail, things like that? I'll be in shortly."

"Okay," I replied. "I'm not all that hungry, but I do have a lot to tell you. Come in soon."

I went back inside and threw myself down on our bed still dressed. I was uncharacteristically exhausted.

"Getting old," I said to no one and closed my eyes.

When I opened them again, Swash was standing over me smiling.

"It must have been a rough day."

"It was an amazing day," I answered. "But there's

a lot to process after a full day at Metropolitan. Let's talk in the living room."

By the time I'd changed, Swash had poured me a glass of beaujolais.

"Okay," said Swash, sipping his wine. "Let's hear it."

"Well, we found the receiver," I began.

"And was it where Jon predicted?"

"Exactly. Just below Shauna's room in a funny little basement under the old wing."

"Jon's a pretty bright guy."

"Yeah, I'm going to consult with him whenever I need to commit a crime."

"Or solve one?"

"That too," I conceded. "Anyway, we tested it out. I turned on the receiver, Shauna uncovered the lens of the camera, and sure enough, there was her room in full view on the screen."

"So now you know how. You just have to figure out who. Maybe Jon could help you with that too."

"Or maybe we can figure it out ourselves." I poured myself some more wine. "No papers to grade tonight, thank goodness, and a guest speaker in tomorrow's class. But wait, there's so much more news!"

Swash passed me a plate of cheese and crackers. "Here, this will help wash down all that wine," he said with a wry smile.

"Thanks." I took a cube of cheddar. "So while

Shauna was checking out the camera, I found this door in the basement, and when she got back, we opened it...."

"And where did it lead?"

"To a sub-basement in the old wing. And we found a desk filled with books and papers that Shauna thinks belong to Leo."

"So you think Leo's been hiding out there?"

"It looked as though it's been his headquarters for some time. Long before Louise was killed." I described the folder with the travel brochures.

"That's actually pretty creepy," Swash said.

"It certainly is. I'm thinking that he's been using the sub-basement for years and years. He had the desk well organized for teaching his courses. And you know, as I think about it, the first day I was at Hilliard High, Shauna and I saw him right near the door to the old basement. That was my introduction to Leo Loops."

"A fateful day."

"So we called the police," I continued. "That young police officer who interviewed me at the Loops's house came to the school, and we showed her what we'd found."

"And was she sufficiently impressed?"

"I'm not sure. We couldn't really prove that it was Leo's desk."

"There wasn't anything with his name on it?"

"Not a thing. And it wasn't clear whether Leo was

still using it as a hiding place." I drained the few remaining drops of wine in my glass. "Officer Archambault seems to have her own theory." I described how she had quizzed me about Amelia and the finding of the body.

"Wow. She thinks Amelia killed Louise Loops?"

"Maybe. Or Amelia helped Leo do it. That certainly seemed to be what she was implying anyway."

"So what exactly do you know about Amelia Rafferty?"

"Well, I know from Elaine that Amelia's from Hilliard and from old money, just like Leo. Her husband works with Warren Dodgson in Hartford. They were good friends — Elaine and Amelia — until Elaine's divorce."

"Not such good friends, if it ended with Elaine's divorce," he said.

"True. But you know how those things go. Amelia's husband has to work with Warren every day. It makes it hard not to choose sides."

"And what about Amelia and Leo?"

"Well, besides having grown up in the same town, Amelia and Leo were longtime colleagues at the high school. So there's a lot of shared history."

"But that would mean Amelia would have known Louise all those years too."

"Yes, that's so," I acknowledged. "Still, suppose Amelia and Leo had somehow fallen in love after being friends and colleagues for ages, and they decided to run away together. Perhaps Leo had been unhappy for a long time, and he'd been planning to leave. Then he persuaded Amelia to help him."

"So Leo killed Louise, and she was dead before you got there?"

"Or maybe Leo had already gone into hiding, and Amelia killed her after we got there?"

Just as Officer Archambault had done, Swash took me through the series of events that had led to my being there when Louise's body was found.

"It certainly sounds like you could have been set up, Susan. Did Amelia know in advance that you would be there that day?"

"Yes, Shauna told her I would be visiting her classes."

"So that might have been the opportunity that Amelia and Leo were waiting for — a complete outsider who could be a witness to the finding of the body."

I winced. "So you think I was an accessory to murder?"

"Some might call you a dupe," he said.

Seeing my horrified look, he added, "Or maybe Amelia's completely innocent. Come on, let's have supper."

"Okay, but I'm afraid I won't be able to eat much. I keep getting flashes of Amelia swinging a one-iron — and she's in Leo's basement, not at the country club."

CHAPTER TWENTY-SEVEN

The next week passed slowly and uncomfortably. Nanette and I ironed out the problems with the physics department, and the plans for next year's schedule went to the dean's office. My classes continued to go smoothly, but I couldn't shake the feeling that Amelia had made a fool of me.

Swash was too excited about his upcoming car show to take my situation very seriously. I thought several times of phoning Elaine to discuss it, but I knew she was in rehearsal for the fall play. I'd have to wait till our Tuesday night dinner.

* * * * *

"Amelia? Never. Not ever," protested Elaine.

This was our first time in Café Lisbon, a Portugese restaurant in the nearby city of Albion, which had been recommended by some of my colleagues at Metropolitan. It was a little place in a strip mall, conveniently close to campus. With large portions and low prices, it was a great favorite with both faculty and students. On this particular evening, a group of rowdy students were in the bar celebrating the latest football victory or the end of midterms or maybe the joys of being young and irresponsible.

"But you haven't seen her for years," I shouted over the din. "You can't say what she's capable of. Would you have predicted that Leo Loops was a murderer?"

"Well, of course not. But I can see Leo as a murderer more easily than I can see Amelia being swept off her feet by Leo."

I might have had some doubt about Elaine's insights into other people, given her blind spot about Jonathan, but I reminded myself that it was just that — a blind spot. She was usually an excellent judge of character.

"So you don't think she used me as her dupe?" I asked, still smarting from Swash's suggestion.

"Her what?"

"Her dupe," I shouted.

"Oh, dupe. No, not Amelia. Amelia's a what-you-see-is-what-you-get sort of person. Very straightforward. Very upright."

"But if she were doing it for love...."

"No, not for love of Leo." Elaine shook her head vehemently. "She might be loyal enough to Leo to withhold some information from the police, but she wouldn't have knowingly involved you, a perfect stranger."

I shrugged. "Okay, you know best. Now what should we order?"

"Order?"

"Yes, what looks good?" I raised my voice a few more decibels.

"The *Alentejo* soup sounds interesting, doesn't it? Garlic and cilantro, and a poached egg on top."

"I'm not so sure about the poached egg," I replied. "I think I'll go straight to the *Mariscada da casa.*"

"I'll order the soup and ask them to put it into two bowls, and I'll take the egg," she said. "I'm going to get the grilled chorizo."

The waiter came to our table and we shouted our orders to him. Elaine added a bottle of *Monte Velho* as an afterthought.

"We're going to need it, if these students don't leave soon," she said.

The wine came quickly, and as we polished off our first glass, I told her about finding Leo's subterranean headquarters.

"Creepy," she said with a shudder. "But think how close you were in your guess about his hiding in one of those fugitive slave sites. And there he was in the underbelly of Hilliard High!"

"Creepy is what everyone says," I replied. "But I love 'underbelly.' No one but you would use that term."

Elaine smiled at my praise, but then her face grew serious. "And having fantasies about Japanese girls —

that's beyond creepy. That's disgusting."

A raucous laugh and a loud cheer came from the bar.

"Maybe that means the party's over," I said.

Just then two bowls of soup, one topped with a congealed egg, arrived at the table.

"No matter," Elaine answered, spooning up the egg. "We'll just eat and yell."

"Mmm, the soup is delicious. Good choice."

"Sure you don't want some egg?"

I shook my head. I was starting to wish we knew sign language.

"Well, enough about Leo," she said. "How's Swash doing with the Bel Air?"

"He's getting ready for the fall car show. He polishes and cleans it constantly."

"Just when is the big event?"

"This Saturday, as a matter of fact. They've rented the Hilliard fairgrounds. Would you like to go? I'd love some company."

"Only if I can bring Jon."

"That might work well," I admitted. "Jon could gush about the cars and that would leave you and me free to walk around and look at the people."

"Jon doesn't gush."

"Of course not. My mistake. Will you accept 'enthuse'?"

"Yes, that's better. Jon is good at enthusing."

"Then it's a date? Saturday morning?"

Elaine nodded just as the waiter reappeared with our entrees. I took one last spoonful of soup and handed him my bowl.

Another cheer rose from the Metropolitan students.

"Oh, to be young again," I said.

"I don't know about that. I'm enjoying this phase of life a lot."

"I guess I am too. Though I'm not the giddy romantic that you are." I took a deep sniff of the garlicky vapors emanating from my seafood. "Mmm, good stuff."

"Well, it may not be romantic exactly, but your life certainly is exciting. Are you close to catching Shauna's phantom?"

"Close, yes. But not close enough. I haven't thought of a way to trap him or her yet."

"Well, you know how he's doing it, so all you have to do is catch him in the act, right?"

"Easier said than done."

"Another chance for Jon to help you, perhaps?"

"Maybe," I reluctantly admitted. "I'll be sure to ask him about it on Saturday."

"Look, they're leaving at last." Elaine waved good-bye to the Metropolitan students who were tossing dollar bills and change onto the bar as they filed noisily out.

We both sighed in relief, then attacked our entrees with new zeal.

"I think we'll just have enough time for flan and decaf," Elaine said. "With a big serving of peace and quiet."

CHAPTER TWENTY-EIGHT

Saturday morning dawned bright and sunny. When I awoke, Swash was in the shower singing "Get Your Kicks on Route 66." I pulled the covers over my head and tried to block out the sounds. It didn't work.

By the time I was dressed, hot bagels were on the table and the coffee was poured.

"Elaine and Jon will be here in ten minutes," Swash said. "Should we all go in the Bel Air? Or take two cars?"

"I'm sure Jon will want to ride in the Bel Air," I replied. "But maybe we should take two cars in case Elaine and I need to make an escape."

"Are you sure you really want to go to this?"

"I definitely want to go. I just might get bored a little sooner than you and Jon."

I had just finished breakfast when Elaine and Jon, both in jeans and suede jackets, appeared on our doorstep. They too had decided that two cars would be best. Jon and Swash headed off in the Bel Air, and Elaine and I followed in Jon's Audi.

"I love to drive his car," she confided. "It makes

me feel so proprietary."

When we arrived at the fairgrounds, Swash turned off at the gate marked 'Exhibitors' while Elaine followed the signs for public parking. Once we'd parked the Audi, we set out in search of Swash and Jon.

It was an overwhelming display. More than a hundred cars were lined up in five rows, their hoods open for inspection. The first few rows we approached were mostly new cars with proud young owners standing beside them. A large crowd had gathered around a glistening green car, which a printed sign identified as a Shelby Cobra.

"It's a limited edition," the owner was saying. A dark-haired man in his thirties, he was clearly enjoying the attention. "Only about six thousand Cobras are manufactured a year."

"How much did it set you back?" asked a younger man in a Metropolitan sweatshirt.

"Forty-seven thousand," the owner replied. "But I just had to have one."

"I wonder what he does to get that money," whispered Elaine as we moved on. "That's a lot of money for a student."

"Well, we know from Swash's experience that you don't have to be a Metropolitan student to join the club," I said. "And he certainly can't be on the faculty — no one could buy that car on a professor's salary."

When we arrived at the two rows of classic cars,

we found Jon standing in front of a low-slung silver sports car.

"It's a Lamberghini," he said in hushed tones.

"It's amazing," I said. I meant it. I'd never seen a car so beautiful.

"Swash is at the end of the next row," Jon said, his eyes still fixed on the car.

Elaine put her arm through Jon's and stood gazing at the car with him. I continued down the row.

Swash, encircled by a group of admiring students, was explaining about the Bel Air's fuel-injected engine. Not wanting to interrupt, I waved as I strolled by. A yellow Jaguar caught my eye and I stopped to examine it.

"You've got good taste," said Jon, coming up behind me. "That's a '52. Doesn't get much more classic than that."

"It's gorgeous," I agreed. "Where's Elaine?"

"She's gone to get us all some coffee."

"Good idea. It is a little chilly today." A red convertible was the next one in the row. "That's a Mustang, right?"

"Yup. It's a '64 and a half, I think. Nice, huh?"

"Mm-hmm. And that one?" I pointed to the dark blue car just past the Mustang.

"Is this a quiz?" Jon asked.

"No, I'm just trying to learn a little more about these things."

Actually, it was a quiz of sorts. I was curious

whether Jon really knew about classic cars or had studied up to impress Swash the first time they met. I was relieved to find that his knowledge seemed to be genuine.

"That's a Pontiac LeMans. About the same vintage as the Mustang. So far, Swash's Bel Air and the Jag are the oldest cars in the show."

"Is there a prize for oldest car, do you think?"

"I'm not sure. We could go look at the trophies. They're on display right near the refreshment stand."

"Okay," I agreed. "I hope Elaine is still there. I don't want to miss her."

"There was a pretty long line for coffee and doughnuts when we came in. She's probably just getting served about now."

Elaine was passing the trophy table when we saw her. She was carrying a little cardboard tray with four coffees and a pile of doughnuts.

"Look at those trophies!" she exclaimed. "That one's 'Best in Show' — just like a cat or dog show."

I read the inscriptions on some of the others: Best Ford, Best Chevy, Best Sports Car.

"Which of these would Swash's car qualify for?" I asked. "Best Chevy?"

"I think that's for newer cars," Jon said. "Here's one for best car, fifty years or older."

"Oh, the Jag's going to get that, I bet. I hope Swash won't be too disappointed if he doesn't win anything."

"Don't worry," said Jon. "Swash can handle not winning. Not eating is another story. I'm going to take him a coffee and some doughnuts. Why don't you ladies just sit over there on that bench?"

"An opportunity to people-watch," Elaine said. "One of my favorite activities." She pointed at the people streaming through the entrance gate. "They don't look like college students though."

"Probably people who just live nearby in Hilliard and want something fun to do on a nice Saturday morning."

We sipped our coffee and shared a jelly doughnut. To my surprise, I was enjoying myself. Everyone seemed to be in a festive mood, and I thought I recognized a few students from Hilliard High.

"I think that's one of Shauna's seniors," I said as a tall boy walked by with his parents. "I remember him reading Chaucer aloud in class. Yes, that's Gabe, I'm pretty sure. He's got a blog that Shauna read to me. It was about Leo and all the supposed sightings of him."

As if to confirm my identification, the boy smiled and waved at me as he passed.

"Seems like a nice kid," said Elaine. "I guess most of them are."

"Yeah, they're a great bunch of kids," I agreed. "Except for the Phantom."

The doughnuts were disappearing quickly and Jon had still not returned.

"Oh, there's Silas. He's the custodian at Hilliard High." I pointed out the bearded man to Elaine. "I think I mentioned him to you. Who's that he's with? He looks familiar too."

I looked more closely. A boy in a Red Sox baseball cap. I did know him. It was Travis, the boy who had been so interested in *Pudd'nhead Wilson*. Why would he be spending Saturday morning with the school custodian?

CHAPTER TWENTY-NINE

"That *is* strange," agreed Elaine when I explained to her who Travis was. "Kids from Hilliard don't hang out with janitors."

"That's what I thought. What can that be about?"

"You don't think there's some kind of impropriety going on?"

I turned to her. "What do you mean?"

"You know, drugs, sex. How else do upper middle class kids get into trouble?"

"We don't know it's trouble. Maybe Silas is a great auto mechanic and Travis is learning about fixing cars from him."

I looked at them again. They were standing next to a shiny new sports car and talking intently. Neither of them seemed to notice me.

"But here's another idea," I said. "Travis is one of Shauna's students. And school custodians have keys. I wonder...."

"Why would a kid like Travis be interested in the custodian's keys? Wait a minute — you think Travis is the Phantom?"

"I think he might be. Befriending the person who has all the keys to the building is a great way to get in and out of classrooms and basements. Not to mention sub-basements."

We were still watching the unlikely pair when Jon returned. Elaine explained our latest theory.

"Could be," he said. "But how do you know that Silas isn't a relative of some sort?"

"Kids from Hilliard don't have relatives who are janitors," said Elaine.

"Elaine, you don't know that," he protested. "Even Hilliard families can have black sheep. Need I remind you about Leo the murderer?"

"Not the same thing," she argued. "Murderers come from all social classes. Janitors don't."

"Does it matter?" I asked, watching as Silas and Travis disappeared into the crowd. "Whether or not they are related, the point is that Travis is hanging out with Silas. And Silas has keys. The real issue is how to find out if Travis is the Phantom."

"You're right, Susan," Jon said. "I think you and Shauna have simply got to catch him in the act."

"That's not going to be easy," I said. "We'd have to keep the videocamera uncovered and the receiver plugged in, so he can start using it again."

"But will he use it again?" asked Elaine. "He must know you're on to the camera arrangement since you covered up the lens."

"If the Phantom doesn't pull another prank, I don't think you'll ever catch him." Jon shrugged. "Maybe that's okay though. You've stopped him."

"But I want to know who the Phantom is," I said. "I think he should make amends for what he's done to Shauna."

"I'd talk to Amelia," said Elaine. "She probably knows all about Travis and whether he's a likely candidate for the Phantom."

"And whether there are any black sheep in his family," Jon added.

Still unsure that Amelia was innocent of complicity in Louise's death, I reluctantly agreed to talk to her the following week.

"Time to see how Swash is doing," I said.

We walked back to Swash and the Bel Air. He was again surrounded by worshipful undergraduates.

"He's not going to need much consoling if he doesn't win a prize," whispered Elaine as we approached. "Look how much fun he's having!"

It was true — Swash was loving the attention. Elaine, Jon and I stood in the crowd and listened to him describe the merits of his car, its engine, chrome and paint job. I basked in vicarious pride until my growling stomach reminded me that it was lunchtime.

"I'm going to get some hot dogs and drinks for the four of us," I said. "Anyone want to come?"

"I will," said Elaine. "You won't be able to carry

everything yourself."

We joined the long line at the refreshment stand. The irresistible aromas of french fries and grilled meat grew stronger and more tantalizing. As we waited, Shauna's student Gabe walked past us carrying a tray full of Cokes and burgers.

"Hey there," he said. "You're Ms. Thompson's friend, right? I thought I recognized you on the bench before."

"Mm-hmm. And this is my friend, Elaine Dodgson. She was Ms. Thompson's favorite teacher at Wintonbury."

"Wow. My favorite teacher's favorite teacher?" He looked down at his tray of food. "I'd shake your hand if I had a free one," he said.

"Don't worry about it," Elaine reassured him. "So are you enjoying the car show?"

"Yeah, it's great. I'm going to write all about it on my blog tonight."

"I've read your blog," I said. "About Mr. Loops being a modern day Robin Hood."

Gabe smiled sheepishly. "I was kinda joking about that," he said. "But it was cool to think of him that way."

"It was good writing," I said. "You made me almost believe it."

"I'd like to believe it myself," he replied. "Rather than think of him as a guy who offed his wife." His face reddening, he looked down at the food again. "I gotta get these to my 'rents."

"Nice meeting you, Gabe," said Elaine.

He mumbled some goodbyes and hurried away.

"His blog really is funny," I said. "But I hadn't put that together with how much the Hilliard students must be freaking out about the possibility that their Mr. Loops is a murderer."

"The school probably put in extra counseling sessions for the students. That's what they always do when something gruesome happens," said Elaine. "For the faculty too, I bet."

We finally reached the front of the line and placed our order. As we carried the food back to Swash and Jon, I noticed people starting to gather at the trophy stand.

"It looks like the award ceremony will be starting soon," I said to Swash.

He looked at his watch. "We've got about fifteen minutes. Now let's see about these hot dogs...."

Jon and Swash downed their hot dogs as if they hadn't eaten in a week, and I confess I wasn't far behind them. Elaine was a bit daintier, but soon all four of us were ready to join the crowd forming near the trophies.

The award that Swash was eligible for was one of the last to be announced. I silently practiced a condolence speech while we waited and held my breath when the president of the car club announced "Best classic car, fifty years or older." He paused and squinted at the name. "Michael Buckler, '57 Bel Air."

We cheered so loudly as Swash walked up to receive his trophy that people turned to see who was making the noise. I could see a look of shocked recognition on the faces of a few of my students, but I didn't mind making a spectacle of myself. My husband was a winner.

CHAPTER THIRTY

We expect each student to become a knowledgeable person who uses strategies and skills across the curriculum and in extra-curricular areas.

— from the Mission Statement of Hilliard High School

That night all four of us went out — in the Bel Air, of course — to celebrate. By the second glass of champagne, I found myself really enjoying Jon's wit. I even thought it was funny that he kept referring to me as Kinsey Marple.

Sunday, on the other hand, was a headachy blur, with classes to prepare and papers to grade. I called Shauna early on Monday morning and asked if I could come by after school.

When I arrived at Shauna's classroom, she was sitting at her computer.

I checked that no one else was in the room. Then I looked up at the videocamera and saw that it had been rewrapped with black paper. "I think the Phantom is Travis," I said.

"Travis? Travis Melton? The guy in my American lit class? I can't see him doing those pranks."

I explained about seeing Travis with Silas at the car show, and what a good resource a custodian was for anyone who needed a key.

"There are lots of reasons he might go to a car show with Silas," she objected. "But I see what you're saying. I suppose it's possible."

"How could we test my theory?" I asked.

She thought for a moment. "We've got to talk to Amelia," she said.

"That's what Elaine suggested." I didn't share with Shauna my concerns about Amelia and Leo. *No use starting unfounded rumors*, I thought.

"Of course, Amelia has a lot to contend with right now," she added. "There are all sorts of rumors circulating about her and Leo."

I sighed. Of course there were. It was a high school.

We found Amelia sitting alone in the English office. I told her about seeing Silas and Travis together.

She pursed her lips. "It's possible, I guess. How is he in class this year? I haven't taught him since he was in ninth grade."

"He's bright," Shauna replied. "When he gets involved with the topic, he's great. But he gets distracted easily."

"That makes him no different from hundreds of other students at Hilliard High," said Amelia. "So the only reason to suspect him as the prankster is his connection to Silas?"

"It seems that way," I admitted.

"But Travis has been here for two years, and he hasn't gotten into any trouble before this, right?" Shauna said.

"True," said Amelia. "But you weren't here till this year, were you?"

I glanced at Shauna, who was avoiding eye contact.

"Amelia doesn't mean this is your fault, I'm sure," I said quickly.

"No, of course I don't," Amelia replied. "I'm just saying that perhaps Travis has developed a love-hate thing for Shauna. You know, he's got a crush on her, but he can't express it and it comes out in these bizarre pranks."

"Do you know anything about Travis's family?" I asked.

"I remember meeting his mother at Parents' Night two years ago. She's some kind of high-powered corporate attorney, I recall. They had just moved into Hilliard the summer before, and I don't think there was a father in the picture."

"So Silas could be a surrogate father," Shauna said.

"Maybe," replied Amelia. "But instead of all this speculation, how about we check Travis's schedule and see if he's free at the times when some of those pranks occurred." She swiveled her chair so that she was facing her computer.

A few taps and clicks later, Amelia had pulled Travis's class schedule up onto the screen. Shauna and I read it over her shoulder.

"That's interesting," said Shauna. "He has the same free periods I have on Tuesdays and Thursdays — third and fifth."

"But that must be true of at least ten percent of the school," Amelia said. "It makes it more likely, but it still doesn't prove anything."

"I suppose I could go through the schedules of all of my students and see if any of the others have similar schedules," said Shauna.

"But they wouldn't necessarily have to be free both periods," I said. "Can you remember what period it was when you and I found the love poem? Or the chess board? He would have to be free the periods before you found those things."

"Let's see. We found the love poem right before my seniors were discussing the Wife of Bath, right? I remember because I was having trouble concentrating on Chaucer with that damn Ethiope verse in my head."

"You certainly didn't show it," I said. "That was a great class."

"And the chessboard appeared while we were at lunch," she continued. "Right after the *Pudd'nhead* class."

"So was Travis free both those periods?" I asked.

Shauna flipped through her plan book and then checked his schedule on the screen. "It would appear that he was."

"Is this enough evidence to confront him with?" I asked.

Both Amelia and Shauna shook their heads.

"There must be something else we can look at," I said.

Amelia tapped her fingers impatiently on her desk, while Shauna and I stared helplessly at the computer screen.

"Wait," I said. "Didn't you tell me that when kids had a free period they had to go to the cafeteria and either study there or sign out to another room?"

"Yes, that's what they do," replied Shauna.

"Well, suppose we look at the sign-out book and find where Travis said he was going during those periods."

"He could have lied," she said.

"True," I said. "But maybe we can catch him in those lies. Where's the sign-out book kept?"

"It goes to the main office at the end of the day,"

Amelia said. "I'll go get it and bring it up here."

While Amelia was retrieving the book, Shauna consulted her daily planner. "I did 'The Wife of Bath' with the seniors on September eighteenth and the *Pudd'nhead* class was on October tenth."

Amelia returned with the sign-out book. "Here we are," she said, handing it to me.

I turned to the page marked September 18. "Fifth period, right?" I ran my finger down the signatures. "Here it is — Travis Melton. Oh, for goodness sake!"

"What?" Amelia and Shauna asked in unison.

"I knew we were dealing with a real master criminal," I said, trying unsuccessfully to keep a straight face. "Look. He's signed out for Shauna's room."

CHAPTER THIRTY-ONE

"You've got to be kidding!" said Shauna.

"Nope. Here it is on October tenth too. Travis Melton signed out for room 208."

Amelia chuckled. "Unbelievable! He does all that elaborate planning. He writes poems, buys subway tokens and hides videocameras — and he can't think of a better place to sign out to?"

"Never underestimate the shortsightedness of adolescents," I said.

"I know. I shouldn't be surprised after all these years," she replied. "I've seen them do far more stupid things, but this prankster seemed so clever."

Shauna was shaking her head. "I can't believe it's really Travis. He seems like such a nice ordinary kid. Do you think he wanted to be caught?"

"No," I said. "He just never figured on anyone checking the sign-out book."

"And I'm not sure we've caught him exactly," said Amelia. "I think we have to confront him with our suspicions and see what he says in his own defense."

"I'd love to be a fly on the wall when you two do

that," I said.

A sly smile slowly spread across Shauna's face. "There's no reason why you can't be — if you don't mind watching television in a musty old basement."

"I love it!" I said. "When?"

"Let's put it off for a couple of days," Amelia suggested. "I need some time to gather more information about Travis. At the very least, I want to talk to the guidance department and see if they can shed any light on his behavior."

"Will you tell them what's happened?" asked Shauna.

"No. I'll just tell them I'm concerned about his distractedness in class, and see what they have to tell us."

"Suppose we schedule the showdown for Thursday afternoon," Shauna said. "I know Susan's usually available on Thursdays."

I checked my calendar. "Right. I'm free. And if I weren't, I'd still get here somehow. What time should I arrive?"

"I'll ask him to stop by during fifth period. We know that he's free then. And that will give us third period to make sure that the camera and receiver are working."

"I'll be here by third period," I said, returning the calendar to my handbag.

"Good work, Sherlock," Amelia called as I headed out the door.

* * * * *

"Sherlock?" said Swash. "I don't know about that. It seems to me that the Moriarty of Hilliard High School wasn't much of a challenge."

"You're right," I said. "He's not exactly a Napoleon of crime. It's pretty funny, isn't it? He did all those amazing pranks and then didn't bother to cover his tracks."

"I'm sure he never thought that anyone would think to look at the sign-out book. Why should they, unless they suspected him?"

"And why would anyone suspect him? He did everything else with such sophistication that we even thought it might be a teacher, not some eleventh grader in a baseball cap."

Swash gave me a crooked smile. "I know I couldn't have pulled off pranks like that when I was a junior in high school."

"But were you in a love-hate relationship with your English teacher? Maybe you just lacked the necessary motivation."

"Ha! I never felt anything but fear or indifference for any of my English teachers in high school. They were all over fifty-five and wore those big old lady shoes. And they droned on and on about symbolism. But I had this pretty, young biology teacher...."

"Yes, Miss Perkins. I remember. That's why you

liked biology — even before you met me."

"Right," he said. "You have her to thank for that."

"Thank you, Miss Perkins. I hope you've had a long happy life, wherever you are. Now how am I going to get any work done between now and Thursday? I don't think I'll be able to concentrate on anything else."

"Hmm. I have a few ideas about ways you might spend some time. I thought they were really good ways to spend time when I was in high school too...."

* * * * *

Amelia was waiting for me in Shauna's classroom when I arrived at Hilliard on Thursday.

"Shauna's gone to the office to get the key to the basement," she said. "I just took the black paper off the camera lens again." She pointed up at the videocamera.

"So have you two planned out what you're going to say?" I asked.

"I know Shauna has something worked out. I'll just be there for support. I think she can get a confession out of Travis on her own."

"Yes," I agreed. "I'm sure she can. She was pretty intimidating even when she was Travis's age." I didn't mention that Shauna had gotten a killer to confess when she was a Wintonbury student. "So what did the counselors have to say about Travis?"

"A lot actually. Remember how you asked about his family? Well, the head of guidance told me that no one is supposed to know about it, but Silas is Travis's uncle."

"You're kidding! I can't believe it." So Jon was right again. Damn.

"I know. I had trouble believing it too, but if you look closely you can see the family resemblance, especially around the eyes. Of course, the beard hides a lot."

I pictured both of them as I'd seen them at the car show. Now I knew why Silas had looked familiar when I'd met him.

"He's Travis's mother's brother," she continued. "She's a lawyer, as I told you, but he's never amounted to much. He moved to Connecticut after a stint in the army, and he's had a string of low-level jobs ever since. Since Silas and Travis have different last names, Mrs. Melton thought no one had to know. "

"Does Silas live with them too?"

"No, Silas has his own apartment over by the reservoir. You know those little garden apartments?"

"Yes, I've driven by there once or twice," I said. His little apartment probably took a big chunk out of Silas's paycheck, but I knew that for Hilliard it was considered 'affordable housing.'

It reminded me of what Gabe had written in his blog about the difficulty Robin Hood would have finding any poor people in Hilliard.

CHAPTER THIRTY-TWO

*We expect each student to become
a responsible citizen who demonstrates respect
for self and others in a
diverse community.*

— from the Mission Statement of
Hilliard High School

I pulled my jacket closed and buttoned it up to my neck. It was colder in the basement than I'd remembered. But then the other times I'd been down here, Shauna and I had been moving around; now I was seated expectantly in front of the TV screen waiting for the Shauna/Travis showdown.

Shauna and Amelia were seated at Shauna's desk and the camera was aimed so that I could see them, and eventually Travis, in profile.

My glance wandered off to the sub-basement door

and I thought again about Leo. But then the sound of the door opening in Shauna's room brought my attention back to the screen. Travis walked into the frame, still wearing his baseball cap.

"You wanted to see me?" he began. As he took in Amelia's presence, he stopped. "Whoa. Am I in trouble?"

"Maybe, maybe not," replied Shauna. "Have a seat, Travis."

I saw him flinch at the 'maybe,' but he sat down. There was a long silence while Shauna studied his face.

"What?" he said at last.

"So Travis, do you play chess?"

"Uh, a little. Why?"

"Just trying to get to know you a little better, that's all."

He fidgeted in his chair. "So why are you here, Mrs. Rafferty?"

"Just observing," Amelia said, as if that made perfect sense.

"Oh. Okay, yes, I play chess sometimes. There's a chess club that meets on Wednesday afternoons, and I go occasionally."

Shauna picked up a pen and wrote briefly in a small spiral notebook. "Interesting. Do you spend much time online?"

"Online? Sure, doesn't everyone? But not that much."

"Uh-huh. Do you buy stuff online?"

"Now and then."

"Ever use eBay?"

"Once or twice. Why?" He crossed his legs and shifted his weight in the chair.

Shauna wrote another note and looked up. "How about writing? Do you like to write?"

"You mean for classes?"

"No, outside of class," she said.

"Not much. I don't have a blog like Gabe, if that's what you mean." He looked down at the floor.

"What about poetry? Ever write a poem?" She looked intently at him.

Even with the less than perfect reception on the TV, I could see Travis's face turn red.

"Poetry? No, I don't think I ever...."

"Do you know what the word 'Nubian' means?"

"I — I don't think so. Can I go now?"

"Have you ever looked at the books on that shelf?" she asked, indicating the paperbacks at the back of the room.

Travis turned his head to look at the bookshelves. I could see the pain in his face.

"Sure, I — hey, is that camera on?" I watched his mouth drop open as he realized that he had made a slip. He stood up suddenly.

"Camera?" Shauna asked. She smiled at him sweetly. "Now how could you know about the camera?"

"Sit down, Travis," commanded Amelia.

He dropped into the chair. "Busted," he said.

* * * * *

At a pre-arranged signal from Shauna, I turned off the television and, giving one wistful look at the door leading to the sub-basement, trotted up the stairs. When I arrived at her room, Shauna was pointing to Travis's signature in the sign-out book.

"Why's she here?" he asked, looking up.

"Dr. Lombardi has been helping us with our investigation," said Amelia. "She may have some additional questions to ask you."

"Three against one," he said. "Not fair."

"I don't think playing mean tricks on a new teacher is exactly fair either," I replied.

"Especially *racist* mean tricks," added Shauna.

"Racist? I'm not racist. I thought it was cool that we finally had an African-American teacher at Hilliard. And I wasn't trying to be mean." He paused. "Although I guess some of what I did might have seemed mean. I'm sorry, Ms. Thompson."

"Apology *not* accepted — yet," she said. "How could you think that calling me a 'token' wasn't mean?"

"Okay, yeah, maybe that was. But the poem was complimentary. And the chess board…."

"Is there anything you want to ask Travis?" asked Shauna, cutting him off and turning to me.

"Yes, there are a few things actually," I said. "First of all, was anyone else involved in these pranks?"

"Involved? You mean did I have help?"

I nodded.

"Well, Zach helped with the poem a little. He gave me the word 'Nubian.' But he didn't know what I was going to do with the poem, so please don't blame him."

"Anyone else?"

"Uh, Jenna showed me how to buy stuff on eBay. But she didn't know why I wanted the tokens, so it's not her fault either."

"And Silas?" I asked.

"Oh god, please don't get Uncle Silas in trouble. He really needs this job." Travis looked as though he would cry any minute.

"So he didn't give you the keys?"

"No way he'd do that. No, I just — uh — borrowed them one day, figured out which one was the master key and had it copied. He never even knew."

I could hear Amelia let out a sigh of relief. She hadn't wanted Silas to be involved either.

"So you're the only one who's really to blame here," I said. "No one else?"

"Yeah, just me." There was a long silence as he brushed the sweat from his brow. "Am I going to get expelled?"

"No," said Amelia. "We're going to deal with this right here. I don't see a need for it to go any further."

She turned to Shauna. "Do you agree?"

Shauna nodded.

Travis looked relieved for a moment, then grew pale at a new thought. "How about my mother? Does she have to find out? Please don't tell her!"

"We'll see," Shauna said. "I need to know something first." She leaned forward in her chair and looked directly into his eyes. "Travis, why did you do all those things to me?"

"I really wasn't trying to be mean — I swear!"

"Then why?"

"I — I don't know exactly. I thought you were cool, cooler than any teacher here, so...." He turned his palms upward in helplessness.

"Did you have a little crush on Ms. Thompson perhaps?" asked Amelia.

"Well, maybe. Sort of," Travis said in a near-whisper, his face growing redder.

"And you didn't know how to express it?"

"Yeah. Yeah, that's kind of what I meant," he answered, not able to look at any of us. "So I wrote that poem about a Nubian princess. And I set up the board with a black queen right after that cool class on Mark Twain. Those were complimentary, like I said before."

"And the upside down books?" I said.

"I guess I was trying to show off — that I knew which authors were black, even though we'd never studied any of them."

171

"And the tokens?" Shauna asked.

"Uh — I think I was trying to say I knew you were the only minority in the school. Isn't that what a token is?"

"And you never thought that this might hurt my feelings?"

He looked at her in surprise. I wondered if he'd ever thought before that teachers might have feelings. "I guess I didn't think it through."

"Let me ask you this, Travis," she said. "Have you ever felt like an outsider anywhere?"

"Sure," he answered. "When I first got here to Hilliard. Everyone else had been to the middle school together, and I had just moved to town and didn't know anyone."

"And how did that feel?"

"It was hard. I just kind of kept to myself and didn't talk and sat alone at lunch. I hated it. But then Zach and I got paired up as lab partners and we hit it off, so things got better."

"How would you have felt if you hadn't hit it off with Zach? If you still felt like an outsider for months and months, maybe your whole freshman year?"

"Awful, I guess."

"And suppose someone had started sending you notes that called you an outsider? Or something worse?"

"I don't think I'd want to come back to school, ever." I watched the light dawn. "I made you feel like that?"

"Something like that," she answered, her eyes welling up with tears.

I think all of us were shocked at this break in Shauna's armor. Amelia and I looked at each other and then at Travis, who was wide-eyed.

"I'm sorry! I'm really, really sorry," he said. "I thought you were so cool. I never thought I could make you feel so bad."

"Your apology is almost accepted," Shauna replied, her voice a bit shaky. After taking a moment to regain her composure, she sat up straight in her chair. "I've been thinking about what you said when we were discussing *Pudd'nhead* and the question of identity. Remember?"

"Um, I'm not sure...."

"You said that you were you because of what you think. You also said it had nothing to do with being white or being from Hilliard."

"Yeah, okay, I remember."

"Well, I disagree. I think being white and being from Hilliard is a big part of who you are, and why you did these things."

"But...."

"Have you ever known anyone who was African-American?"

"No," he said. "And neither have any of my friends. We've talked about that. A couple of kids have Hispanic cleaning women, though."

"I think you need some new experiences in your life," she continued. "I want you to sign up for the after-school tutoring program that Hilliard and a couple of other high schools run in Hartford. You're going to get to know some kids who aren't white and aren't from Hilliard, and then in a few months, we'll see if you think differently."

Travis sighed. "Okay, I'll do that. And then you'll accept my apology?"

"Only if you come and talk to me once a week about what you're doing."

"Okay, I will, I promise. Can I go to the guidance office and sign up now?"

Shauna nodded. "Go ahead, Travis. I'll see you tomorrow."

Travis said his goodbyes and left.

"You were terrific," I said to Shauna and received a radiant smile in answer.

"Simply wonderful," agreed Amelia, putting an arm around Shauna. "We're so lucky to have you here at Hilliard."

"I'm glad you feel that way," Shauna replied, still beaming. "You know, this isn't exactly what I expected teaching English to be like, but it's kind of cool."

CHAPTER THIRTY-THREE

As I drove away from Hilliard High, an uneasy feeling crept over me.

Why should I feel like this? I wondered. I'd discovered the identity of Shauna's Phantom; he had confessed and been brought to justice. I should be elated. And yet, something was nagging at me. I put on a CD of Bobby Darin singing his jazziest songs and tried to make myself feel like celebrating.

It didn't work.

When I came home, Swash was in the kitchen hovering over a pot.

"Chicken Provencal," he said in reply to my kiss on his cheek.

"I really need to talk," I said. "Do we have time before dinner?"

"Uh-oh. I know that plaintive voice. I'll be right there after I put this in the oven and pour us some wine."

I threw my professorial clothes in a heap on the bed and changed into jeans and a turtleneck. By the time I had plopped down on the living room couch, Swash was handing me a glass.

"Okay, what's up?" he said.

I described Shauna's interrogation of Travis, his subsequent confession, and the punishment she'd devised for him.

"She's really something, isn't she?" Swash said with an appreciative smile. "A true force of nature, that Shauna Thompson." He raised his glass in salute. "And here's to you, my brilliant detective. Another case solved."

"But that's just the problem," I said. "I don't feel like celebrating. Something is bothering me, and I don't know what it is."

"Let me zee if za doctor ees in," he replied, trying for an Austrian accent but managing only to sound like Mel Brooks.

"Yes, doctor, and what is your analysis?"

"Well, could it be that you're just sad that you won't be seeing Shauna anymore, now that the puzzle is solved?"

I thought about that for a moment. "Well, I will miss seeing her. And her students."

"But that's not it?"

"No, I don't think so. I'm sure she'd be glad to meet me for dinner sometime, so it's not like I'll never see her again. And I certainly get to visit classes in lots of other high schools when *my* students are out student teaching. No, it's a nagging feeling that I can't quite put into words, even for myself."

"Nagging? Like there's something still left to do?"

"Maybe. But I can't think of what it could be."

"Hmm. Could it be that you feel like you need to repair the Amelia-Elaine relationship?"

"No," I said with certainty. "I know that's not up to me. That's *their* problem. It's something else."

"Something else left to do...."

I sipped my wine in silence. I kept my eyes on the glass but I could feel Swash studying my face.

"Could it be that you really want to solve the Leo Loops thing?" he asked at last.

"Maybe," I admitted. "I was there when Louise Loops's body was found. I *am* involved in that case, at least a little."

"But you don't really know the people — either Louise or Leo."

"That's true, I don't. And Officer Archambault certainly seems competent. I don't know what I could possibly add."

Swash gave a sigh of relief and looked at his watch. "It's time to get the chicken out of the oven," he said, getting up. "Let's talk about something else over dinner. We can watch a movie after that and let your subconscious work on the problem meanwhile."

"Zat's vat you prescribe, *herr Doktor*?" I asked. My Viennese accent was even worse than his.

* * * * *

In keeping with our *mittel Europa* theme, we decided to watch *The Shop Around the Corner*, which was playing on our favorite cable channel. As it faded to a close, something was definitely stirring in my mind but not yet at the surface.

"I love that movie a little better every time we watch it," Swash was saying. "The thing about Lubitsch as a director is that what's unsaid is as important as what is said. Don't you think that scene where Jimmy Stewart — what? Why are you looking at me like that?"

"It was something that was unsaid, I think," I replied. "The thing that was nagging me."

"We're back to Travis and Shauna?"

"Yeah, sorry. Something Travis didn't say, maybe. But something he did say too. Or maybe it was something Shauna forgot to ask...."

"Well, that's a whole lot clearer now." Swash frowned as he pushed the usual multiplicity of buttons on the remote, shutting down all the various pieces of technology. "What's next on the agenda? Is it bedtime for the great detective?"

"In a little while," I said. "I think I'll just sit here and stare at the blank screen until I can make some sense of my thoughts. That was a great movie, by the way. I'm sorry — I guess I'm just distracted tonight."

Swash gave me a forgiving kiss and wandered up to our bedroom.

Something said and something unsaid. Something said: that should be easier. What was it? Had Travis said something we hadn't picked up on? I tried to remember the scene I'd watched on the TV monitor. I could picture Travis's face and hear Shauna asking him about his writing. He had mentioned Gabe's blog. Was that it?

Yes. Why mention Gabe's blog? Sure, Gabe was a good writer but why bring him up? Well, maybe all the students at Hilliard High read his blog, so he was considered a model of someone who wrote frequently and persuasively. Or maybe Gabe and Travis were good friends? But they weren't in the same class; Gabe was a senior and Travis was only in eleventh grade. And when Travis needed help with his poem, he'd asked Zach for help, not Gabe. So why mention Gabe at that point? And why evade Shauna's gaze immediately afterward? I had definitely seen him look away uncomfortably after his reply about Gabe.

Okay, Gabe and his blog: maybe that was the thing that was said that I should have picked up on. Then what was the thing unsaid?

I went to my desk to do a quick search of the Web. With a few clicks, I found Gabe's blog and began to scan it for entries about "Loopy." He had written three more since the original message comparing Leo to Robin Hood. Two were about reported sightings, one near the village green and the other outside the Hilliard ice skating rink (but with no comparison of Leo Loops to Hans

Brinker). The third referred back to the Robin Hood theme:

> I'm thinking again about our own Loopy,
> the bandit of Hilliard Forest. Will he attract
> his own band of bandits? And who will they
> be? Perhaps other Hilliard High teachers will
> join him as an act of solidarity. Anyone know
> the position the teachers' union takes on
> renegade teachers? If the teachers won't join
> him, maybe some of his students will. After
> all, didn't Loopy teach us about Thoreau and
> Civil Disobedience?

Wait a minute. First Gabe had compared Leo Loops to Robin Hood, and now he was writing about students forming a band of Loopy followers. Hmm. Leo Loops had a sub-basement hideaway. And — yes! — Travis had the master key to all the rooms in Hilliard High, including the sub-basement. So perhaps, like me, he'd stumbled across Leo's lair. Was it too farfetched to think that Travis might be helping Hilliard's most famous fugitive? Why hadn't we asked him about the sub-basement when we were talking about the keys?

Obviously, we were too focused on Travis's role as the Phantom. It hadn't occurred to us that he might also be playing another part: one of Robin's Hood merry men.

I hurried upstairs to tell Swash, but he was already asleep. He mumbled something as I lay down beside him.

"It's nothing," I replied. "I just wanted to say you're right. Lubitsch *is* a great director."

CHAPTER THIRTY-FOUR

We expect each student to become a
scholar who gathers information,
assesses the value of information,
and applies previous learning to school subjects
and to life activities.

— from the Mission Statement of
Hilliard High School

Now it was my turn to ask Shauna for a favor. I called Hilliard High the next morning and left a message on her voicemail to get back to me at the university. I was holding office hours — with none of my students in sight — when she returned the call.

"Shauna, I'm so glad to hear from you."

"What's up?" she asked.

I explained my suspicions about Travis's connection to Leo Loops.

Shauna sighed. "Oh no. I hope Travis isn't mixed up with Leo too. Would that make him an accomplice or something?"

"I'm not sure. Let's talk to Travis together and see what he knows. Then maybe we can find a way to get the information to Officer Archambault without naming names."

"I've already seen his class today, but I can probably track him down and get him to stay after school. Can you be here then?"

I checked my calendar: I had only morning classes and there were no meetings in the afternoon. "I can," I said. "Do you think Travis will cooperate?"

I heard her chuckle. "He's very remorseful about hurting me and so grateful that he's not being suspended. I think he'll cooperate."

"See you soon. My car goes on auto-pilot to Hilliard these days." Before she could hang up, I added, "Don't tell him what it's about, Shauna. I think surprise may be to our advantage."

* * * * *

When I arrived, Shauna and Travis were sitting at the front of her classroom. Travis rose when I entered and offered me his chair.

"You remember Dr. Lombardi, right?" asked Shauna.

"How could I forget?" Travis replied with a sheepish grin. He pulled a third chair to the front so we could talk.

"Well, she's got a few more questions for you that she didn't get to last time. You'll be glad to help her out, right? Straight answers?"

He nodded and gave me his attention.

"So, Travis," I began. "You mentioned Gabe yesterday. Are you a fan of his blog?"

"Oh, yeah. He's really funny, and smart too." He looked directly at me, his face full of wide-eyed innocence, but I noticed the color rising up his throat to his cheeks.

"Do you remember the time he wrote about Mr. Loops and Robin Hood?" I said.

"Sure. Gabe's written about that two or three times, actually."

"Yes, I saw those. He made Mr. Loops into a kind of hero in the one I read. Did you think so?" He nodded again. "But I wanted to ask you, have you happened to see Mr. Loops — since he disappeared, I mean."

At this, Travis gave me an incredulous look. "Me? No. Why should you think I would?"

"Well, let me put it this way: when you were down in the basement with the TV monitor, did you ever notice a door at the end of the room?"

"Door?" He was silent for a few moments, furrowing his brow as if he were trying hard to remember.

"Oh, yeah, sure."

"I thought you might have. And did you ever open it with your master key?"

"I — I might have."

Shauna gave him a stern look. "Straight answers, Travis, remember?"

He squirmed in his chair. "Yeah, I opened it."

"And went down the stairs and looked around?" I continued.

"Yeah, I did."

"I did too," I said. "It was irresistible, wasn't it?" He nodded. "And was Mr. Loops there at the time?"

"No." Another silence while he tried to figure out what to say next. "But I did go through the desk and see some of the handouts he used with our class last year," he added.

"So you knew that Mr. Loops had a hideout there, didn't you?"

"Yeah, I figured it out. But I really haven't seen him, like I said."

"Have you been leaving food for him there?"

Travis looked uncertainly at Shauna. "Will I get in trouble?" he asked.

"You'll get in more trouble if you don't tell," she replied.

"Are you going to tell my mother?"

"I think we can keep this just between us," I said. "But you really have to tell us everything you can."

"Okay." He swallowed hard.

"First of all, is anyone else involved?" I asked.

He shifted in his chair.

"Travis...." said Shauna.

"Okay, okay. There are three of us who have been bringing food and leaving it on the desk in that room. I've been bringing mostly Burger King, Zach's been doing McD's and Kathryn brings stuff from the place she works."

"The Hill of Beans," I said.

"Yeah. How do you know that?"

"I saw her there once. But it doesn't matter. What about Gabe?"

"No, Gabe's not involved at all. He just writes about stuff."

"All right," I said. "So as far as you know, it's just you, Zach and Kathryn. Have any of you actually seen Mr. Loops himself?"

"Zach said he did. Once. But not in that underground room."

"Where then?"

"He said he saw Loopy in the woods behind the soccer field one day after practice. It was kinda dark so he couldn't be sure."

"Travis, there's one thing I really want to know," Shauna said.

"Sure, Ms. Thompson. Anything."

"Why, Travis? Why give Mr. Loops food and not

tell anyone where he was, when you knew the police were looking for him?"

"Because we all had him last year for English, and we thought he was a good guy. We just knew he wouldn't murder his wife."

"Why do you think he's in hiding then?" she asked.

"Because *everyone else* thinks he murdered her. And he's trying to find out who did do it — before he gets caught and put in jail."

"That's kind of a romantic vision of Mr. Loops," I said.

"Romantic?"

"Yes, as if he's some wronged hero, and you three are the only ones who really understand the situation."

"Oh, I see. Well, yeah, kind of. We refer to him as Robin Hood when we text about him."

Shauna groaned. "And are you his merry men?"

Travis looked at her. "We do have code names. Zach is Little John, Kathryn is Maid Marian, and I'm Will Scarlett," he said with pride.

CHAPTER THIRTY-FIVE

How can one relatively decent kid get himself into so much trouble, I thought as I drove to the Hilliard police station. I'd left Shauna to deal with Travis and his fear of incarceration and phoned ahead to see Officer Archambault in person.

There was a burly officer on duty at the front desk when I arrived at the gleaming glass and steel police station. 'Officer Foster,' his nameplate informed me.

"Officer Archambault is expecting me," I said.

"Yeah, go ahead," he said, barely looking up from his paperwork.

I found her waiting for me by a coffeepot in a large well-lit room that contained two rows of desks and chairs and little else. Two other officers were there, chatting with her and eating pastries, but they quickly left us alone.

"Have a coffee or a danish?" she asked.

"No thanks," I said.

A ceramic mug in one hand and a cheese danish in the other, she led me to her desk, which was surprisingly uncluttered.

"I've got more information about Leo Loops," I said, taking a seat in the chair opposite hers.

She put down the food and picked up a manila folder.

"Another Leo sighting?" she asked with a faint smile. I could tell she wasn't taking me seriously.

"No, sort of the reverse. I know how Leo Loops is getting food without being seen by anyone."

"You do?" At last, her eyes showed some interest in what I had to say.

"Yes, I do. Some of the Hilliard High kids are taking turns buying food and leaving it in that sub-basement I showed you."

"That's news to me," she said. "We've been watching the high school — I think I told you that. No one has seen him go in or out."

"But you haven't stationed anyone down in the sub-basement?"

She shook her head. "Not enough staff to cover all the places that people claim to have seen him. Maybe we will put an officer down there, though. You say the kids leave food and when they come back it's gone?"

"That's what they said, and I believe them. They didn't give the information up willingly." I wondered if she'd ask how I got them to give me the information at all, but she just sat there, patiently waiting for me to go on. Probably an interrogation trick she learned in the police academy. "So, somehow he's getting in and out of that building without being seen by the police officer who's watching the high school."

"Or he's finding a place to hide *inside* the building that none of us know about."

"One of the kids mentioned seeing him in the woods behind the soccer field," I added.

"The woods?" She leaned toward me. "You're sure that's not just another Leo sighting, like all the rest?"

"I don't know. These kids know him pretty well...."

"Hmmm. Wait here," she said, getting quickly up from her desk. "I'll be back in about five minutes." She strode out of the room.

Through the glass I could see her heading out of the building and across the parking lot to the Town Hall. I tried to be patient as I waited for her return, but it was getting late and Swash would be wondering where I was. And it had been a long day. Well, maybe a danish would make the time go faster, I thought, getting up. Just then Officer Foster came into the room.

"Kris wants you to go over to Town Hall," he said. "The Office of Records."

It took me a few seconds to put "Kris" together with Officer Archambault, but then I realized I had seen her first name on some papers that I had been trying not to read on her desk.

"Okay," I said and followed the path I'd seen her take ten minutes earlier.

She was waiting for me just inside the door marked
'Records.' In her arms were two long rolls of paper.
"Architect's plans for the high school," she explained.

I followed her over to a long oak table and watched
her unroll one of the plans. "This is the original building," she said. "You know how to read one of these?"

"Not really," I admitted.

"Me neither." A sheepish smile broke through her
usually serious manner. "Let me get someone who
does."

I tried to make sense of the drawings. Recognizing
the wing of administrators' offices, I used that to figure
out where the other rooms were. I'd managed to locate
the old auditorium when Officer Archambault returned
with a gray-haired, slightly stooped man she introduced
as Henry McQuillan.

He leaned over the open drawings, one of us on
either side of him.

"Now this is the building they put up in 1920," he
explained. "I wasn't working here then." He winked at
me and chuckled. "Wasn't even born yet, in fact. She's
a nice old building, isn't she? See here's the entrance
with the arch, and here's the principal's office and the
old gym...."

"What about the basement?" I asked. "And is there
a sub-basement?"

"Sure, there's a basement. They wouldn't build a
school without a basement in Connecticut in those

days. Here it is." He pointed at a lower level in the diagram. "Sub-basement? Oh, you must mean the old storage room." His finger, just a little shaky, followed a set of stairs from the basement to a still lower level.

The plans were starting to make some sense to me now as I imagined myself walking down those stairs.

"Is there any way to get into the storage room from outside?" asked Officer Archambault. "Without going through the rest of the building?"

McQuillan looked at her quizzically. "Now why would anyone want to do a thing like that?"

She smiled and shrugged.

"Nope, nothing like that," he said.

He rolled the plans back up, and placed a second set out on the table. "Now this is the addition they added in 1985. All bricks and glass — and no real basement at all, you'll notice. Just like this place, a big glass box." He gestured at the walls around us. "Used to be they made public buildings that were beautiful, majestic, like the old Town Hall. But I'm an old man — what do I know about modern architecture?" With a sigh, he let the plans roll back up.

Officer Archambault echoed his sigh. "That's it, huh? No more basements?"

McQuillan straightened up and took the rolls of paper under one arm. His eyes closed for a moment as he tried to picture something. "Wait here," he said and hurried off. He returned a few minutes later with a small roll of paper in his hands and a big smile on his face. "Since you two lovely ladies like basements so much, this should interest you."

He unrolled the paper and stood back to let us look.

The date on the plan was 1952 and it was labeled "Bomb shelter."

"What is this?" asked Officer Archambault, although it was clear from her wide-eyed look that she had a good idea what he was going to say.

"This is the bomb shelter that old man Loops — that was Leo's father — had built and then donated to the town," he replied. "Everyone was worried about the Russians attacking back then, and old Loops decided to protect the youth of Hilliard."

"Does it still exist? Where is it?" I asked, certain I knew the answer.

"Well, there was one attached to the elementary school, of course. But they tore that nice old building down. They probably left the bomb shelter in the ground when they razed the building, because no one remembered it was there. And there's one attached to the high school too. It's located just under the woods behind the —"

"Soccer field?" I asked.

"Yes, that's right. How'd you know?"

"And it would attach somehow to the high school?" Officer Archambault asked. "Underground?"

"You two are some smart ladies," said McQuillan, shaking his head. "Yes, there's a narrow tunnel that goes from the shelter to the basement, or maybe it's the storage room...."

CHAPTER THIRTY-SIX

I stood outside the police station watching Officer Archambault drive off in her cruiser. The two officers whom I'd seen talking to her at the coffeepot followed closely behind in another police car. I fumbled in my handbag for the little notebook in which I'd written down Shauna's cell phone number, found it and called, hoping she might still be at the high school.

"Hello?"

"Shauna, where are you?"

"In my classroom. Travis was here for a while after you left, and I decided to stay and set some stuff up for tomorrow. I was just about to close up the room and go home."

"I think you may want to stay around a bit longer," I said. "The police are on their way to pick up Leo."

"Leo! Where?"

"In a bomb shelter that opens up in the woods behind the soccer field."

"You mean where Zach saw him?"

"Exactly. And it connects to the sub-basement by a tunnel of some sort."

"A bomb shelter — I didn't think they had those anymore."

"They don't. In fact, they'd forgotten this one ever existed. Listen, I want to meet you. Where's a good place to meet where we won't be in the way but we can see what's going on?"

"I bet they're going to clear the building and the surrounding area before they go after him," she said. "Why don't I meet you on the corner of Wintonbury Road and Montgomery Lane — or as close as the police will let us get to that corner."

"See you there in a few minutes." I ended the connection and quickly phoned Swash.

"I'm going to be a little late, honey," I said.

"What's up?" he asked.

"The police are picking up Leo and I want to be there to watch."

"What?!! Susan, did you have something to do with their finding him? And what do you mean by 'watch'?"

"I mean just that: watch. They won't let me go near enough to be in any danger, I promise you."

"I hope so. Okay, I'll keep the lasagna warm, but I'll expect a really good story with supper when we finally get to eat it."

* * * * *

Shauna had been right. The building had been cleared, and police were blocking cars from all the roads surrounding the high school. I found Shauna standing with Silas on a corner a block away from our planned meeting place. A small crowd of Hilliard citizenry had begun to gather.

"We were the only two left on the second floor," Shauna explained after I'd greeted both of them. "I don't know if anyone was still in the first floor offices. Anyway, we got a polite but firm police escort from the building." She paused for a split second. "Damn."

"I know," I said. "I wanted to see them get him too."

People of all ages were streaming out of their houses to join the group. Shauna recognized a few students and nodded to them, but she stayed close to me, clutching my arm. An elderly couple had come out of their big colonial on the corner and were peering at the school through binoculars. I craned my neck but couldn't see anything except the outlines of the high school in the dusk and the glare of flashing police lights surrounding it. I could hear the words "Leo Loops" on everyone's lips. Weeks of waiting and wondering were soon to be over — or at least that's what everyone hoped.

"It's him! They've found Leo Loops!"

"It's about time. What do we pay their salaries for?"

"I haven't felt safe in my own house for weeks with that Loops on the loose."

About an hour passed. It grew dark. With the addition of more and more people, the gathering was taking on a party-like atmosphere. A few television stations had sent cameras and reporters. Students were laughing and shouting to each other, talking into cell phones and sending text messages. A few had brought burgers and cokes for their friends. My stomach growled at the smell.

Shauna said, "I've got some Altoids in my bag. Want one?"

As I started to express my gratitude, we heard a siren. Soon a few hundred eyes watched while an ambulance was allowed through the police barricade.

"Someone's hurt," went the word through the group.

"They shot him!"

"Leo's dead!"

"Poor Loopy!"

"Pigs!"

"You don't know that! Any of it!" Shauna shouted into the crowd.

Some of the other adults joined her in quieting the growing furor. About ten minutes later, the ambulance screamed out of the high school driveway and onto Wintonbury Road, heading toward Hartford.

"Okay, everyone go home," said an officer who had been assigned to keep us behind the police lines.

"What happened?" someone demanded.

"Go home," he said. "It'll be on the eleven o'clock news."

There were groans of disappointment, but the crowd began to disperse.

"Where's your car?" I asked Shauna.

"Just around the corner. Where's yours?"

"A few blocks down."

"I'll give you a ride," she said.

We trudged toward the side street where her car was parked. Before we got there, a police cruiser pulled up. Officer Archambault was at the wheel and she waved us over. Her face was grim.

Shauna spoke first. "Did you get Leo? Is he okay?"

"Get inside," she answered. "You might as well know what's happened. It'll be on the news in a few minutes anyway."

Shauna and I clambered into the back seat of the cruiser.

Officer Archambault turned in her seat to talk to us. "He's dead," she said. "Hung himself from the light fixture in the shelter."

"Oh god," I said.

"Poor Leo," said Shauna.

"Yeah, it's sad. Finding suicides is a part of this job that I hate."

"So what happened?" I asked, trying not to sound too eager.

"Well, some of the guys tried to find the entrance

199

to the shelter in the woods, but it was covered up with brush. Three of us went into the high school and down to the sub-basement where you had showed me that desk. We looked for an entrance to the tunnel — it was pretty hard to locate."

"But you obviously found it," I said.

"Yes," she replied. "That desk of his was sitting over it. That's why we couldn't see it. We moved the desk, and there was a trap door. There was a big hand-written note *on* the desk, by the way. All it said was 'They know.' I think one of the kids was trying to warn him."

Shauna and I exchanged glances.

Officer Archambault looked at us curiously but didn't ask us anything. I got the feeling that she didn't want to pursue it. "We got out flashlights and followed the tunnel," she continued. "It was creepy. Narrow, and low enough so the taller guys had to bend over, and full of broken cobwebs and mice. Someone had clearly been using it. It went on for about a hundred feet."

Shauna and I listened in silence, though I could feel her shivering next to me as Officer Archambault told us the story.

"Finally we got to the door, which wasn't locked. We went in, guns out, and there he was, hanging from the overhead light. It wasn't a pretty sight. Our radios didn't work from inside there, so we had to find the door to the woods and go up the ladder to call the ambulance. Loops hadn't been hanging there long, I could tell, but I didn't think they'd be able to revive him anyway. And they couldn't."

"Was there a note?" I asked.

"Yes," she said. "He'd scrawled it on a piece of paper torn from some spiral notebook. It said, 'I wanted adventure. She wanted to die in her home. So I pushed her down the stairs.'"

CHAPTER THIRTY-SEVEN

Shauna and I sat there too stunned to speak.

"That was it," Officer Archambault said. "Two lives gone because your Leo wanted some adventure."

"So sad," murmured Shauna.

He wasn't my Leo, I thought, but I decided it best to hold my tongue.

"So you two had better be going home now. Thanks for your help. Both of you." She sounded sincere, but it was clear that Officer Archambault wanted to go home herself, or at least back to the station.

We climbed wearily out of the back seat. Huddling together beneath a streetlamp disguised as an old-fashioned gaslight, we watched the cruiser drive off.

I turned to give Shauna a hug goodbye.

Since she was almost a foot taller than I was, it was a bit awkward, but she responded warmly. "Thanks, Susan — for everything."

"I know we'll see each other again, Shauna. Please stay in touch."

"Of course, I will. But didn't you want me to drive you to your car?"

"Huh? Oh for goodness sake, I thought we *were* at my car. I guess this whole day has been a little disorienting. Sure, I'll take you up on your offer."

"It's going to be quite a day at Hilliard High on Monday," I said as Shauna started up the engine.

"TGIF. At least the parents get to deal with it over the weekend, before the school has to do its part. I bet the kids are going to be freaking out, not to mention the faculty."

"Especially Amelia."

"Oh my god, Amelia. I'm upset, and I only knew him a month or so. She's going to be distraught. And the kids who had him last year...."

"Travis and Zach and Kathryn — they thought he was too nice a guy to kill someone. How are they going to handle this? Poor Travis already has so much on his conscience."

"Well, we'll just have to help each other through it, I suppose." We drove in silence for a minute. "This one's your car, right?"

"Yes, it is. Goodbye again, Shauna. I hope I'll see you soon."

She gave a tired little wave in response and drove off.

* * * * *

I was barely in the door when I heard the beep-beep-beep that meant Swash was reheating my dinner in the microwave.

"Here, sit. You must be famished," he said, hovering in concerned-spouse mode. "But after the first couple of bites, you have to start telling me about it."

"Thanks, sweetie," I said, gratefully digging into the lasagna.

Swash joined me at the table and waited patiently.

"Okay," I said after a few more mouthfuls of pasta and green salad. "First of all, they found Leo — but only after he'd hanged himself."

"Holy shit," he said. "Please tell me that *you* didn't find the body."

"No, I didn't. Remember I told you that they cleared the area and cordoned it off." I explained about the bomb shelter and the tunnel to the sub-basement. "I think Officer Archambault told Shauna and me some of the details because she was grateful that we had helped the police locate Leo. But she's too much of a professional to let us bumbling amateurs anywhere near a possible crime scene."

"Thank goodness for the professionals," he replied. "So was there a suicide note?"

"I'm coming to that. Just one more little helping...."

Over coffee, I described the contents of the note.

"So he was bored with his marriage and he wanted adventure," said Swash. "That's a reason to murder your wife? He couldn't just go skydiving on weekends? Take a trip to Antarctica next summer?"

"Or collect '57 Bel Airs?" I asked.

"Hey! I'm not the one who gets involved in murder investigations, am I? I'm not looking for adventure. And I didn't get the Bel Air because I was bored with my marriage."

"Well, I'm glad to hear that," I said. "But in Leo's case, you're forgetting his fantasy about the Japanese women. I don't think Louise would have approved of that quite as easily as she might have gone for Leo's taking a trip to Antarctica."

"That's true. So then he could have divorced Louise, married someone younger and more exotic — like Warren Dodgson did. You didn't see him murdering Elaine."

"Elaine! I wonder if she's heard about Leo."

"I guess you should give her a call before it gets too late. I'm amazed she wasn't waiting on our doorstep when you got home."

"I bet she's gone to New York to see Jon and hasn't heard about any of this. She probably left right after school this afternoon."

Sure enough, there was no answer at Elaine's house. I left a message on her machine to phone me at work on Monday, since I knew she'd be getting back too late Sunday night.

With so little left of the evening, Swash and I decided to settle in for a movie, something as far from

Hilliard and Leo Loops as we could find. I chose *The Band Wagon* with its show business story, lush Technicolor, and bright witty music. As Fred Astaire led Cyd Charisse into their "Dancing in the Dark" duet in Central Park, I heard Swash sigh.

"What is it?" I asked. "Anything wrong?"

"No," he said. "Just the opposite. I'm the anti-Leo."

"Me too."

"And, for the record, life with you is never boring. In fact, maybe we could do with a little less excitement?"

CHAPTER THIRTY-EIGHT

Elaine phoned me Monday afternoon in the midst of my office hours.

"I saw the article on page three of the *Courant* this morning," she said. "I hadn't had time to catch up with the weekend's papers yet, but I dropped everything and fished out Saturday's front page. My god! Leo a murderer — and a suicide!"

"And living in a bomb shelter. Don't forget that."

"We've got so much to talk about. Where shall we meet tomorrow night?"

I groaned. "I haven't had time to find us a good place. I've been kind of involved with the stuff at Hilliard."

"I bet you have. How about trying Federico's? I've heard some good things about the food there."

"That's the one that opened last summer on Route 10? Where Scarlett O'Hara's used to be?"

I heard Elaine chuckle. "They do come and go, don't they? Yes, that's the one. See you tomorrow at seven?"

* * * * *

Elaine was uncharacteristically early and waiting for me at a table near the back when I arrived at Federico's.

"No strolling guitarists," she said. "No piano-playing relatives."

"And no celebrating college students," I said. "So we're off to a good start."

"Let's order right away so we can really concentrate on talking," Elaine suggested. "I can't wait to hear all about Leo."

The menu was full of appealing dishes but I quickly settled on a seafood and pasta specialty — *frutta di mare alla Federico*. Elaine ordered veal marsala and a bottle of pinot grigio.

"Okay then, what didn't the papers tell me that I should know?" she asked.

I explained about Travis and the other two Hilliard students who were bringing Leo his meals.

"You mean that nice girl who served us at The Hill of Beans?"

"Mm-hmm. Kathryn was Maid Marian. As well as Goth girl — I think I told you about that?"

She nodded. "So these kids were supplying him with food, I get that. But the newspaper said he was living in a bomb shelter. How did the police ever figure that out?"

I described Mr. McQuillan and his set of building plans for the school.

Elaine took a sip of the wine, while the waiter hovered. "Very good, thanks," she told him. "Now that you mention it, I do remember Leo's father — Edwin Loops — was a bit of an alarmist when it came to the Russians. I think he had a bomb shelter built for the Loops mansion too. I wonder why Leo didn't just stay in that shelter."

"Well, for one thing, his house was probably being watched more closely than the high school."

"That makes sense," she said, nodding. "The *Courant* also mentioned a suicide note, but they didn't reveal the contents. Did you get to see it?"

"No, though I do know what was in it." I repeated what Officer Archambault had told us.

"Adventure!" she said, gnawing angrily on a breadstick. "All he really wanted was to have an adoring young woman who would think he was God, even if it meant he had to travel halfway 'round the world to find one. As if that could compensate for being a failed writer. Men!"

"Hmm," I said. "Do I detect a bit of disillusionment with Jon in that statement?"

"Huh? No, of course not. Jon's not like other men." She smiled contentedly. "But we'll talk about him later. Let's finish with Leo."

"I think I've told you everything. What are *your* thoughts? You knew Leo and Louise, after all."

"I keep thinking about poor Louise. She didn't

deserve to die, no matter how boring she was."

"Of course not. Leo had to be really unbalanced to think that was the only way to end the marriage. And everyone seemed to think they were such a happy couple."

"Who knows what goes on in someone else's marriage," Elaine mused. "People probably thought Warren and I were happily married. Hell, I did too."

"That's what Amelia said, almost word for word. That we never know about other people's marriages."

"Amelia! She must be so dreadfully upset about this. Maybe I should call her...."

"I bet she'd really like that," I said. "She seemed to feel guilty about how your friendship ended. And she said she missed you."

"Well, she should feel guilty. But still, I think I *will* call her. We'll have plenty to talk about."

As our main courses arrived, I thought back to Amelia and some of the other people at Hilliard. "You know, it's funny. Even with what we said about not truly understanding other people's marriages, there were a lot of people at Hilliard who had an inkling about this." I described the teachers' online bulletin board and the posts about going to Tahiti and the South Seas "sweeties."

"He must have given himself away in little things he said or did," Elaine replied.

"Yes, even those young teachers in the history department, who couldn't have known him all that well, had theories that were pretty close to the truth. One of them said Leo needed to break free of all that domesticity and go after his last chance at adventure. That's almost exactly what he wrote in his suicide note."

"Well, there you are. It was only a surprise to people like Amelia and me, who thought we knew him." Elaine looked at me curiously. "And how is Swash these days?"

"Don't worry, Elaine. We're doing fine. Swash isn't going anywhere, and neither am I."

"Glad to hear it. How's your seafood?"

"Delicious," I said. "The sauce is just spicy enough." I took another bite. "I'd like to come here again. It's quiet, and the waiters are attentive, but they leave us alone to talk."

"My veal is superb too. I think the décor could be improved — too much red velvet and gold — but at this point, we should be grateful to Federico, whoever he is, for providing us with a meeting place."

"Well, that's one thing settled for a while."

"Until they close it down and replace it with a hot dog stand," she said.

"And what's the latest with you and Jon?"

That contented smile again. "Ah, I was waiting for you to get back to that. We're great, absolutely made for each other. He's talking about moving up here, in fact."

"Up here? You mean he's getting his own place in

Connecticut? Or are you saying he's going to move in with you?"

"With me, of course. He'll still keep the apartment in Manhattan as a *pied de terre* for the two of us. It's perfect."

I did my best as a friend to be happy for her. "Perfect," I said.

"We might even get married at some point," she continued.

"Elaine! After all you've said for years about men and marriage, you'd actually consider that?"

"Face it, Susan. No matter what the odds are, people will keep getting married."

* * * * *

Weeks went by, and the events at Hilliard High started to fade, both from the headlines and from people's thoughts. The Christmas season was fast approaching. Swash planned to do all of his holiday shopping online, but I decided to pick up a few gifts at the Hilliard mall. I needed small presents for the half dozen teachers who had allowed my students to observe in their classrooms that semester.

I looked at over-priced boxes of chocolate and sweetly scented candles and bought a few of each. As I strolled out of the candle store, I saw someone walking ahead of me who, at least from behind, looked just like Shauna. But this woman was walking hand in hand with a dark-haired young man about the same height as she was. Could it be the Yale grad student?

There can't be too many people who look like Shauna, even from the back, I thought. I hurried to catch up to them.

It was Shauna. And the young man was Jonah.

"Hey, Doctor Lombardi," said Jonah, letting go of her hand.

"Susan, I'm sorry I haven't been in touch," said Shauna at the same time. "It's been so hectic."

"That's okay. I remember what my first year of teaching was like. It's great to see you both. How is Hilliard High surviving?"

"Some of the kids and teachers are still shaken," Jonah replied. "Especially the ones who thought they knew Leo well. But kids that age are pretty resilient, aren't they?"

I nodded. "How about Travis?"

"He's doing well," Shauna answered. "He's really involved with the tutoring program, and I think that's helped him recover from the Leo mess faster. He's even convinced Zach to join the program."

"And Kathryn?"

"Goth as ever, at least in school. I think dressing like that is her way of showing overprotective parents that she's her own person. They won't let her do any tutoring because it's in Hartford."

"And Amelia?"

"She's bounced back. She was pretty depressed for a while, even more than she let anyone see, I think, but now she's in life-goes-on mode and full of ideas for next semester."

"Well, send her my regards," I said. "And say hi to Travis for me. I still think of him and his pranks now and then."

"We will," Jonah assured me. I noted with interest the way he said 'we'.

"Well, I'll let you two get on with your shopping," I said. "I'm sure I'll return to Hilliard High one of these days. And I hope I'll see you both under more pleasant circumstances than the last time I was there."

"Oh, you will," said Shauna. Gazing at Jonah with affection, she added, "Circumstances at Hilliard actually have gotten very pleasant."

I gave them each a hug and watched them walk away, hand in hand once more.